Even the Score

by Belle Payton

Simon Spotlight

New York   London   Toronto   Sydney   New Delhi

SIMON SPOTLIGHT
An imprint of Simon & Schuster Children's Publishing Division
1230 Avenue of the Americas, New York, New York 10020
This Simon Spotlight edition January 2015
© 2015 by Simon & Schuster, Inc. All rights reserved, including the right of reproduction in whole or in part in any form.
SIMON SPOTLIGHT and colophon are registered trademarks of Simon & Schuster, Inc.
Text by Heather Alexander
Cover art by Anthony VanArsdale
Design by Ciara Gay
For information about special discounts for bulk purchases, please contact Simon & Schuster Special Sales at 1-866-506-1949 or business@simonandschuster.com.
The text of this book was set in Garamond.
Manufactured in the United States of America 1214 FFG
10 9 8 7 6 5 4 3 2 1
ISBN 978-1-4814-1952-9 (hc)
ISBN 978-1-4814-1951-2 (pbk)
ISBN 978-1-4814-1953-6 (eBook)
Library of Congress Catalog Card Number 2014935213

CHAPTER ONE

This is no big deal, Ava Sackett thought. Then she turned and sprinted away from the boys.

Her heart beat in rhythm with her feet. Thin lines of sweat trickled down her neck from the heat of the September Texas sun. Her fingertips tingled with anticipation. She sensed the coaches on the sidelines watching. *Today is my big chance,* she thought. A chance to show she could do more than kick a football.

She was now the official kicker of the Ashland Tiger Cubs. She was also the first girl in the history of Ashland Middle School to make the football team.

Not that any other girl had tried out.

She knew some boys in the halls had been whispering about her. They said that her being on the team was a pity thing or a special consideration, because her dad coached the high school team. Her twin sister Alex told her not to listen to them.

"You're good at football. *Really* good. Better-than-most-boys good," Alex insisted. And when Ava kicked the thirty-three-yard field goal at the game last Saturday, those boys finally stopped whispering.

"I'm going to try mixing things up," Coach Kenerson announced at practice today. "Ava, you go in for Ethan at wide receiver."

She couldn't hold back her grin. Finally! A chance to be a part of the action.

Wide receivers needed to be superfast to catch the pass from the quarterback and then sprint down the field for a touchdown. Running wasn't a problem for Ava. She'd always been fast. Her mom said she ran before she learned to walk. Ava flexed her fingers, readying herself for the catch.

Corey O'Sullivan, the quarterback, torpedoed the ball toward the other wide receiver, Owen Rooney. Ava wished Corey had sent it her way, but he'd made the right choice. She was sur-rounded, while no defenders blocked Owen. It was an easy grab-and-go.

Ava watched the ball land in Owen's out-stretched hands. Then he pivoted his shoulders suddenly, and just as suddenly, the ball dropped onto the grass. Defenders dove in for the inter-ception.

"Are you kidding me?" Coach K bellowed. He threw up his stocky arms in disbelief. Owen, their star wide receiver, had bungled the easy play.

Again.

Coach K marched across the field until he stood an inch away from Owen. He pressed his face close to Owen's helmet. "What is with you this week? These are Pee Wee catches. Baby stuff. Where's your focus?"

Owen shrugged and stared at his cleats.

Even across the field, Ava saw Owen's face flame. His wiry body tensed as the coach yelled. Ava felt bad for him. Owen was usually able to catch the trickiest passes, but his technique had been sloppy all week.

As Coach K returned to the sidelines, Owen glanced toward her. She met his gaze, hoping to send some silent encouragement. She and Alex always did this across a crowded room, and it worked.

Must be an identical twin thing, Ava decided, because Owen scowled at her, then turned away.

Ava jogged back to the line of scrimmage. Was Owen angry that Coach K had also put her in at his position? She'd moved to Ashland, Texas, from Massachusetts this summer and didn't know Owen well enough to know how competitive he was.

They ran the drill again. Ava sprinted into the backfield, hoping to find an open pocket. She heard defenders alongside her. Her focus stayed on Corey as he set up for the pass. Once again, he targeted Owen.

Ava's gaze moved to Owen. For a split second, she thought he glanced back at her. She shook her head. That couldn't be right. A wide receiver would never take his eyes off the ball.

Then Owen stumbled. He caught himself quickly, but not before the football landed five feet behind him.

Coach K paced the sidelines, muttering loudly. Corey jogged over to Owen. "What's the deal, O? Those are perfect passes I'm sending you."

Owen shrugged, then snuck another quick glance toward Ava.

Corey kicked at the grass. This was the closest Ava had ever seen him come to losing his cool. "Come on, O! Work with me."

"Rooney!" Coach K called. "Move yourself to tight end."

"But Coach, I always play wide receiver on the left," Owen protested.

"This time you're not." Coach Kenerson blew his whistle. "Get in alongside Sackett."

Owen hurried next to Ava. She tried to catch his eye, maybe give him a thumbs-up or something, but now he wouldn't even look her way. The whistle sounded, and the center snapped the ball. Ava took off. Owen raced alongside her, keeping pace.

They matched each other in speed. Ava tracked the arc of the football while her feet stayed in motion. The ball headed toward her. Her heart pounded with anticipation as she readied to make the catch.

If she nailed this, maybe Coach K would put her in more games. Up until now, he'd been nervous about having her on the field where she could get tackled. That girl thing again! But she wasn't afraid. Her dad and her older brother, Tommy, had taught her how take a hit. Plus, she was fast. These boys had no chance of catching her once that ball was cradled in her arms.

Come on, come on, she chanted silently as the ball soared toward her. She sensed Owen only inches away, hovering by her side. Why was he so close? Didn't he trust her to make the catch?

She squinted into the sun and reached up. As her fingertips brushed the ball's worn leather, something hooked her ankle. Her feet flew up, and she landed with a surprising thud on the ground. Her stomach twisted as the ball rolled out of reach.

An incomplete pass.

She whipped her head around. Owen was sprawled next to her, his cleat suspiciously close to her ankle.

"Did you trip me?" Ava asked.

"S-sorry," Owen stammered. He pulled away from her. "I got too close."

Before she could reply, Coach K towered over them. His mirrored sunglasses hid his eyes. "Rooney! Sackett! Are you two confused?"

"Confused?" Ava repeated.

"Did you think this was a clown routine at the circus?" He ran his fingers through his graying hair. "Do you need me to draw a picture to show you where the wide receiver and tight end are supposed to run?"

"I know where to go," Owen insisted, standing.

"Me too." Ava scrambled to her feet as Coach Kenerson lectured about playing position.

She waited for Owen to tell the coach that it was his mistake, that he'd accidentally tripped her. Owen stayed silent, and Ava fumed. Or maybe it wasn't an accident. Had Owen messed her up on purpose?

"Let's run it again," Ava suggested. She was eager to prove herself.

This time Corey sent the ball right to her. She caught it easily, dodging the defenders nearby.

"That's how it's done!" Coach K cried. "Everyone give me two cooldown laps around the field."

The team set off jogging. Ava and Owen pulled off their helmets and joined the pack.

"Hey, Owen! Want a candy bar?" Xander Browning called loudly.

"Huh?" Owen asked.

"I've got plenty of Butterfingers. Oh, wait, you don't need any of those today, do you?" Xander teased. A couple of guys laughed.

"That's not funny," Ava called back. All players had off days. And off weeks.

"Peanut butter with chocolate is my favorite kind of candy. How about you?" she asked Owen, even though she knew the crack was about his failure to catch and not about a candy bar. She thought he'd appreciate her changing the subject.

He opened his mouth as if to say something. Then he scowled and sprinted forward. He finished half a lap ahead of the rest of the team.

Owen really doesn't like me, Ava realized. She wondered why. She usually got along with guys who played sports. Her sister said she "spoke their language." But Owen wasn't speaking to her at all.

Ava gulped from her water bottle and wiped her forehead with a towel. Her short chocolate-brown curls lay matted in sweat. Helmet-head was way worse than regular hat-head! As she tried to fluff them with her fingers, she overheard Ryan O'Hara, the tackle, and Andy Baker, the middle linebacker, behind her.

"Owen looks horrible out there," Ryan complained.

"It's all her fault," Andy whispered.

Ava stiffened. She didn't have to guess who they were talking about. She was the only girl on the field.

"My dad and brother said this is what happens when you let girls play. My brother said they're bad luck on the field," Andy reported.

"You're right!" Ryan sounded as if he'd just discovered a big secret. "She's messing him up."

Ava swallowed hard. She wasn't doing anything to mess up Owen. He was messing up all on his own.

Getting on the team hadn't been easy. She had had to appeal to the school board to give her a fair chance. Now that she'd made it, she just wanted to be like everyone else on the team. She didn't want to be the *girl* football player.

This is Texas, she reminded herself. *People here don't like it when outsiders mess with their football traditions. Girls aren't part of the football tradition.*

Coach K had them gather around and take a knee. She gazed at her teammates. Corey gave her a grin. Most of the guys, like Corey and Xander and their friend Logan Medina, supported her. Big, burly Andy never said anything nice about anyone, so she wasn't surprised that he had a problem with her. She glanced at Owen, always so cool and mellow. She never thought he'd be angry to have her on the team.

". . . we have one job every Saturday," the coach was saying when she tuned back in. "What is it?"

"To win!" they all cried.

"Wrong!" bellowed Coach K. "Our job is to play our best as a team. A team is a group effort. So if you had a bad day, got a bad grade, ate a bad sandwich, that's your deal and you need to leave it behind in the locker room. When you walk onto this field, you walk on as a group. We have a job to do together, so you have to all stop thinking about yourselves and put the good of the team first. Am I clear?"

"Yes, Coach!" they all shouted.

"Great. Tomorrow I expect you to come to practice with better focus and ready to play as a family. Together we will light up that new scoreboard we're getting!"

The team all placed their hands in the middle and yelled, "Go, Cubs!"

Ava chewed her lip as she made her way off the field. Coach K was right. Her dad was always telling his players the same thing. She was too caught up with proving herself. She had to stop worrying and do what was best for the team.

From now on, she'd be a total team player.

Alex Sackett tapped her purple pen against her new notebook. She glanced at the red, blue, green, and orange pens lined up neatly by her arm. Her plan had been to take meeting notes in different colors. Blue for calendar dates. Green for fund-raising events. Red for money issues. Orange for seventh-grade notes.

She loved color-coding. She arranged her underwear drawer by color. It drove Ava crazy. Ava's drawers had no order. Her underwear was tossed in with her sweatshirts and outgrown bathing suits.

But what should she use the purple pen for? Alex hadn't decided yet.

"Alex, will you take the minutes today?" Ms. Palmer, the student council adviser, asked.

"Sure thing!" Alex smiled. Purple would be

for writing down the minutes! She turned to a blank page. She loved blank notebook paper. The possibilities to fill it were endless.

She glanced to her left at sixth-grade president Chloe Klein. Chloe had turned over a math worksheet to scribble notes with a pencil that was missing an eraser. Next to Chloe, eighth-grade president Johnny Morton leaned back in his chair and stared out the window. He hadn't bothered to bring paper or a pen to the after-school meeting. A baseball player who'd broken the school's pitching record, Johnny had an easy smile for everyone. All the kids liked him, and he'd definitely won off his popularity.

No wonder Ms. Palmer chose me to take notes, Alex thought. Of the three class presidents, she was definitely the most organized. In addition to the presidents, the vice presidents, secretaries, and treasurers from each of the three grades filled the classroom Thursday afternoon for the student council meeting.

Alex took a lot of notes and made a lot of lists. Her family teased her for it, but she tried to explain to them that her lists were calming, that they gave life order. She listed vocabulary words to learn, hobbies she wanted to try, exotic places to visit, books she'd read, and movies she'd watched. When she was little, she kept a running list of her favorite animals and quizzed her family weekly on it. Ava was the only one who knew when giraffe had switched places with dolphin.

"First item," Ms. Palmer announced. "We will be hosting the Homecoming dance in the gym next month, and we need to start planning. Who has ideas for a theme?"

Chloe raised her hand.

"No hand raising here," Ms. Palmer said with a smile. "This isn't a classroom." She glanced at the desks and whiteboard and chuckled. "Okay, it *is* a classroom, but we're not in class. We're having a discussion. Everyone can just talk, as long as we all listen, too."

"How about Texas Sky?" Chloe suggested. "We could decorate with glow-in-the-dark stars."

"I like Hollywood Nights," the eighth-grade vice president said.

"We could have a red carpet leading into the gym," added the sixth-grade treasurer. "And wear movie-star dresses."

Everyone had an idea. Alex thought the girls' ideas were much better than the boys'. One sixth-grade boy wanted the theme to be Extreme Sports.

"How would you decorate the gym?" she asked him.

"Zip lines," he answered. "And skateboard ramps."

"But the girls want to wear pretty dresses," Alex protested.

Idea after idea was presented, and Alex had something to say about each one. Her mother liked to say she skipped baby talk and started speaking in full sentences, every one stating her opinion. Not all of her comments were negative. She liked a lot of the ideas, especially the Hollywood one. She felt good about speaking her mind. *This is why the seventh graders elected me,* she thought.

"Okay, let's revisit the list at our next meeting," Ms. Palmer announced. "Now on to planning our annual car wash."

As Ms. Palmer reviewed the details of the big car wash to raise money for student activities and equipment, Alex wondered about the dance. Back in their old town in Massachusetts, the middle school didn't have dances. She'd never been to one. What would she wear? She imagined herself in a shiny, hot-pink dress she'd seen in a fashion magazine. Her long, curly brown hair would fall to her shoulders in soft waves. She would look so good in that dress walking into the dance with . . . with who?

Her heartbeat quickened. Who would she go to the dance with?

She glanced around the table. No one on the student council interested her. She couldn't stop picturing Corey O'Sullivan in a dark suit and a pink tie to match her dress. He'd look so good. *They'd* look so good.

She shook her head. There was no way.

Alex was pretty sure Corey was going out with Lindsey Davis again, and she and Lindsey were on their way to becoming close friends. Weeks ago she'd chosen Lindsey's friendship over Corey, even though it seemed like Corey liked her. But now he was back with Lindsey. So who could be a potential date?

"Alex," Ms. Palmer called. "Can you read back the budget figures?"

Alex glanced at her notes and read back the numbers. Her purple pen hadn't stopped writing, even while she daydreamed. Ava could only focus on one thing at a time. Not Alex. She did her homework, watched TV, and texted all at the same time and never missed a word.

Ms. Palmer reported that last year the student council had raised two thousand dollars through car washes, bake sales, and T-shirt sales. "This money is buying a new electronic scoreboard for the football team," she announced proudly. "Once I send in the payment, the scoreboard will be delivered and installed next week."

Everyone clapped.

"We should turn our attention to what to buy with the money we'll raise this year," she said. "Ideas?"

"New uniforms for the baseball team," Johnny said.

"The school banner at the football field should be replaced," the Extreme Sports boy added.

"We could pay a celebrity to be at the pep rally for the first game," put in Carly Hermano, who was a cheerleader. Alex had met Carly when she'd foolishly tried out for cheerleading. Alex couldn't get any of the steps right, and she was deathly afraid to try a backflip. Not good for cheerleading! Carly did an amazing backflip and was also the seventh-grade vice president.

"There are other things at this school besides sports," Alex interjected.

All eyes turned to her.

Suddenly she wished she hadn't spoken. She didn't want anyone to think they'd made a mistake electing the new kid as president. But she took a deep breath and continued. "We could plant flowers outside the building. We could buy supplies for the art room or new instruments for the band. We could have the literary magazine printed in color."

"We have a literary magazine?" Johnny asked skeptically.

"Well, if we don't, we should start one," she said. "The point is, we should think beyond the sports field. There's more to Ashland Middle School than football."

CHAPTER TWO

"You're here!" Ava was startled to see her dad the next morning standing by the kitchen counter in his rumpled orange coach's shirt.

"I live here," Mike Sackett said, plunging a tea bag into a mug of hot water. "Remember?"

"Kind of." Ava grinned. "But it's Friday morning. You're always at school super early on game day. Don't you have to nail down some last-minute strategies?"

"I'm trying something new." He took a deep breath. "Relaxation. Meditation. All that Zen stuff your mom talks about."

Ava raised her eyebrows skeptically. "How's that working for you?"

Coach took a sip of the tea and made a sour face. "Totally stressing me out." He tossed the remaining tea into the sink. "I need coffee."

Ava grabbed a blueberry muffin and sat at the table next to Alex, who had already finished her yogurt and was now rapidly flipping through what looked to be vocabulary flash cards. Ava couldn't imagine a worse way to start the day.

"Morning, Mom," Ava called.

Mrs. Sackett raised her arm in greeting from the small kitchen desk, then continued to type furiously on her laptop. Ava wondered if her mom had even gone to bed. When she'd said good night, Mrs. Sackett had been sitting at the computer and wearing the same gray sweatpants. Her long, wavy hair was still gathered in a loose ponytail. Moxy, the family's Australian shepherd, lay under the desk and across the toes of her fuzzy green socks.

"Morning." Tommy wandered in with his hair wet from the shower. He poured a large glass of orange juice, which he chugged in a single gulp. He grunted before pouring a second glass of juice. Tommy wasn't a morning person.

"Let's talk game-day football, Coach," Ava suggested. Mike Sackett's ruddy face brightened.

Nothing made him come alive more than football. "What's the deal with the Ravens?"

"Michael, I thought you were going to take a break from football this morning—" her mother started.

"The Ravens are going to be a challenge." The Ashland High Tigers were on the road tonight against the Ridgefield Ravens. Her dad's green eyes sparkled. Mrs. Sackett sighed.

"Strong offense or defense?" Ava asked.

"Strong checkbook," he answered.

"What does that mean?" Alex looked up from her cards.

"Big money," Tommy explained. He slathered toast with what seemed like half a jar of peanut butter. As sophomore third-string quarterback, Tommy was trying to bulk up, but the massive quantities of food he shoveled in never seemed to stick.

"The Ravens are the wealthiest school we play," their dad explained. "These kids have it all. Fancy uniforms, amazing weight room, high-class trainers, private lessons."

"What about talent? You can't buy talent," Alex observed.

"Or determination," Ava added.

"True," he agreed. "Our team has heart and focus—"

"And mad skills," Tommy finished.

"Indeed." Coach sipped his coffee. "A new weight room would be nice, though."

"The middle school is getting a high-tech scoreboard," Alex said proudly. "Isn't that great of the student council? The scoreboard is digital and does all these cool things."

"What was wrong with the old one?" Mrs. Sackett asked.

"It was old and, uh . . ." Alex hesitated.

"It just told the score." Ava jumped in to help Alex. "The new one will display everything—the number of time-outs, possessions, and stats on all the players."

"But isn't the score all that matters?" Mrs. Sackett asked.

"Always," Coach agreed. "That's what I've been telling my boys. Bells and whistles and shiny new toys don't win games."

"You'll win tonight," Alex said confidently. She stood and tucked her note cards into her school bag.

Ava shook her head. Sometimes Alex acted as if it were so simple to win a football game.

Alex had never been on the field. Plus, Ava had heard that the Ravens had a punishing defense.

"I hope so." Coach drained his coffee. "Got to go. Hey, Laur, should we keep the ice cream thing to the players or invite parents, too?"

Her mom continued to scroll through different web pages. "Huh? Ice cream?"

"The annual Ice Cream Chow-Down," her dad repeated.

"What's that?" Ava asked. Ashland had so many football traditions, it was impossible to keep them straight.

"Next Friday after the game, all the players have an ice cream chow-down at the coach's house," Coach Sackett explained.

"Thirty boys who eat like Tommy are coming here to stuff themselves with ice cream?" Alex wrinkled her nose. "Seriously? We'll need a truckload of ice cream."

"And hot fudge and whipped cream," Tommy added. "Rainbow sprinkles, too."

Their mom groaned. "A chow-down? Hon, you know I'm trying to start up my ceramics business. It's hard to find the time to make the pottery, package and send it, advertise, plus—"

"It's for the team, Laur," their dad interrupted. "They're a big part of our lives now."

"That's just it—" their mom began.

"We'll help," Ava broke in. "Al and I excel at ice cream."

"You know, Daddy, just because you, Tommy, Ava, and this whole town live and breathe football doesn't mean Mom has to twenty-four/ seven too," Alex said. In the short time they'd been here, they'd quickly learned that the team expected more than just coaching from their dad. They also expected a lot more from the family—barbecues, fund-raisers, and apparently, ice cream chow-downs.

"Ice cream is not football," Tommy protested.

"It's better than football," Alex quipped.

"Whoa there!" Coach clutched his hands to his heart, pretending to be horrified.

Mrs. Sackett let out a shriek. "Look at this! Look at this!" She jabbed her finger at the computer screen.

Ava hurried over, followed by the rest of the family. "That aqua bowl is yours, right?"

Mrs. Sackett nodded. "It's featured on my website, but this isn't my site. On this site people post crafts and art that they like. It's called pinning.

Check out how many times my vase has been pinned!"

"Wow! Four hundred forty-six times," Alex said. "Impressive."

"Is that a lot?" Ava asked. She pretty much only watched movies and checked sports scores on the computer. Alex was the social media goddess. She knew everything about every site.

"Huge," Alex said. "And every pin links back to Mom's site. Mom is famous." She reached over and clicked the screen to the web page she'd helped their mom set up. "Check this out. Orders are pouring in!"

Mrs. Sackett squealed. "Oh my God. I *am* famous! And busy! This is crazy!"

Ava was proud of her mom. She used to teach art in their old town, but since they'd moved, she was focusing on her old love, ceramics. Ava couldn't believe how talented she was. Ava could barely draw stick figures.

Mrs. Sackett stood. "Time to get the show on the road. I need to get working—you saw how much work it took to fill my last big order, and that was just for one person! You all need to go to school. And your dad needs to win a football game."

In minutes, their family had scattered.

"So, Sackett, you understand how this tackle thing works, right?" Jack Valdeavano perched on the corner of Ava's desk, waiting for Mrs. Vargas to start math class.

"Tackle thing? What are you talking about?" Ava twirled her pencil between her fingers. Jack was one of her good friends, but talking to him when they weren't shooting hoops made her strangely jittery.

"You need to wait for the tackle to hit you *before* you land on your butt." Jack gave her a crooked grin.

Ava sucked in her breath. "How'd you hear about that?"

"Everyone knows. There's even a video up."

"No!" She lowered her voice. "Really?"

"No, not really. Got you!" Jack pushed back the unruly hair that always flopped into his eyes. "Corey told me."

"Well, it's not funny. Our practices have been horrible this week." She glanced across the room. Owen sat at a desk by the window. He was reading a paperback book, but she couldn't see the cover. "Anyway, what do you know about tackling? You play wimpy sports that don't need pads," she teased.

"Soccer and basketball require skill. We are athletes, not barbarians." Jack smirked. They had a running joke, debating which was better—soccer or football.

"A trained monkey can kick a ball into a goal," Ava scoffed.

"At least it's *trained*!" Jack said, before Mrs. Vargas called the class to order.

Ava tried her hardest to concentrate on the different triangles Mrs. Vargas drew on the board. The teacher was explaining how to find the third angle when you knew the other two.

Right triangles were easy. The other ones confused her. Obtuse. Acute.

Acute was smaller. *How can I remember that?* she wondered. She thought of her last session with Mrs. Hyde, the learning specialist at the school. Ava had been meeting with Mrs. Hyde ever since she'd been diagnosed with ADHD, to help figure out the best ways for her to study. Mrs. Hyde taught her to make up rhymes or come up with a picture that went with the word.

Acute. A cute. Cute.

Immediately her gaze drifted toward Jack.

Jack was cute. Very cute.

She loved his caramel skin and his shaggy, jet-black hair. She loved how thick his eyelashes were. They made his dark eyes look huge.

She shook her head. They'd tried going out on a sort-of date, but it was way weird. Neither of them knew how to act. Afterward they seemed to have reached an unspoken agreement to just be friends. Shoot hoops at the park, watch sports on TV together, that kind of thing.

Ava was glad.

But she still thought he was cute. No, she thought he was *acute*!

Jack listened to Mrs. Vargas and had no idea Ava was staring at him. It figured! Boys were so clueless.

She tried to listen too. Then she felt it.

At first she wasn't sure what exactly. Just a feeling. A sense.

She blinked rapidly and kept her gaze on the board. Mrs. Hyde had warned her about allowing her mind to wander in class. She couldn't let it happen. *Focus!*

Mrs. Vargas called up Megan Schiller to solve a problem. Megan's green marker squeaked on the whiteboard, as she furiously crossed out several false starts. Ava was proud of herself. She knew the answer. She tapped her pencil impatiently, watching Megan fumble her way through.

The feeling was still there.

The feeling of being watched.

Ava dropped her pencil. Then she swiveled in her seat, pretending to search for it. Her eyes darted around the classroom, and she spotted him.

Owen.

He was staring right at her!

Ava quickly snatched her pencil and turned forward. She shook her head. *He wasn't staring. He was probably just spacing out, because watching Megan cross out number after number is torture,* she reasoned.

Mrs. Vargas finally came to Megan's rescue, and then moved on to a different type of problem. More triangles. More mystery angle measurements.

Ava felt his eyes on her again. Was she imagining it? She tried to stay focused on Mrs. Vargas, but curiosity won out. She turned.

He *was* staring! Immediately Owen whipped his head down, knocking his chin against his chest.

Ava turned back. He looked angry. Was he angry at her? She hadn't done anything.

"Okay. Do I have any volunteers to solve this problem?" Mrs. Vargas asked.

Ava barely glanced at the problem. Instead she remembered Coach K's speech. The team needed Owen to be able to catch. Was she making him angry and causing his problems?

"No one?" Mrs. Vargas frowned. "Ava, why don't you give it a try?"

"Me?" Ava gulped and stood shakily. The entire class now stared at her as she made her way to the front. She had no idea where to even start.

And then the bell rang. Saved! She hoped Mrs. Vargas didn't hear her exhale in relief.

"Next time, you're up, Ava," Mrs. Vargas called, as Ava hurried back to her desk to scoop up her books.

Ava chased after Owen. *If I can make him my friend, that'll help the team.*

"Hey." She tapped his shoulder as she caught up with him in the doorway.

He flinched but stopped.

"Can you believe how harsh Coach K has been?" Ava asked, as the rest of the class streamed past. "You know, I don't think it's us. My sister Alex has him for homeroom, and she says he's been really cranky all week."

Soon they were the only ones in the doorway. Owen didn't answer. He stared at her in surprise. Ava plunged ahead. "You know what drives me crazy? His mirrored sunglasses. I can't see his eyes. I think eyes say a lot about what a person is truly thinking, don't you?"

"I, uh . . ." Owen opened, then closed his mouth. The tips of his ears flamed, and he scowled. Then, without speaking, he turned and pushed his way into the crowd, disappearing down the hallway.

What is with him? Ava wondered.

"I don't get it," Ava confided to her friend Kylie McClaire at lunch. "What did I do? Owen acts so weird when I'm around."

"What makes you think you did something?" Kylie asked. "How do you know he doesn't act weird all the time?" Her dark eyes flashed mischievously. She liked sparking a debate. And Ava liked debating with her.

She was glad that she'd found Kylie in this big school. Kylie was cool without being a slave to the popular girls. Everything about her was unique: She wore metallic beads at the ends of the dozens of thin braids that cascaded down her back. Her fingers each sported a different silver ring. Today she wore red jeans and a cropped black jacket. Plus, she lived on a ranch on the outskirts of Ashland.

Last week, when she called Kylie her best friend, her dad was surprised. "Isn't Alex your best friend?" he'd asked her. She'd explained that Alex was her *other half*, which was much more than a best friend. And totally different.

"Okay, so the boy is weird." Ava bit into her peanut butter and jelly sandwich. She'd eaten the same sandwich for lunch every day since kindergarten. She didn't care that Alex had started bringing salads, because she thought they were more grown-up. She liked PB&Js with no crusts, so why change? "I wish he'd stop staring and glaring, though."

"There's nothing wrong with weird, you know," Kylie pointed out. "You don't know what Owen's like at all."

Ava glanced across the cafeteria to where

Owen sat with Logan, Andy, Ryan, and bunch of the other football boys. "I do know he's really fast and intense on the field."

"What about off the field?" Kylie picked at her blue nail polish as she spoke. "Owen's really smart."

"He'd have to be to play wide receiver."

Kylie gave an exasperated sigh. "Ava, he's about so much more than football! Do you know he reads fantasy? And has smart insights on the plots and the characters?"

"No." Ava scrunched up her nose. "How do you know that?"

"We read the same books. And we talk about them almost every night," Kylie said.

"You two talk? How did I not know this?" Ava did a quick mental replay. Sure, she'd suspected Kylie had a little crush on Owen, but when did that turn into late-night book talks?

"Well, not *talk* talk," Kylie admitted sheepishly. "Chat online. We both belong to the same fantasy forum. He uses the screen name OwenRooney. Boys are so literal. But he doesn't know I'm me. He thinks he's talking to ranchergirl722."

"So tell him," Ava encouraged.

Kyle shook her head and peeled a strip of

polish from her thumb. "I can't. I mean, what if I do and then he stops chatting with me?"

Ava stared at her best friend. She'd never seen confident Kylie so unnerved. *She really likes him,* Ava realized.

"I think he would be excited if he found out," Ava said.

"I don't want to risk it. Besides, I don't think he even knows I go to this school," Kylie moaned.

"I can talk to him about you," Ava offered. "I see him at practice every day, and believe me, I'm searching for something to say. I'll talk you up."

"Really?" Kylie's round face broke into a smile. "But you won't tell him about ranchergirl, promise?"

"I promise. I'll tell him how great you are. I'll get him to notice you," Ava pledged.

Kylie hugged her. "You are the *best* best friend ever!"

CHAPTER THREE

Alex fixed her curls in the bathroom mirror, then applied another layer of shimmery gloss to her lips. She stepped back and took a long, appraising look.

Did she look older than twelve? *Most definitely,* she decided. With the chunky necklace over the collared shirt and the cuffed jeans she'd seen the girls at the high school wearing, she could pass for fourteen. Especially with the thick black mascara she'd bought at the drugstore highlighting her green eyes.

She held up silver hoop earrings to her ears. Would these bring her to fifteen? She really wanted to look fifteen today. Totally sophisticated.

Alex slipped them on, thankful that her dad was out for a run. He'd been in a good mood since the Tigers' victory over the Ravens last night, but even so, he wouldn't approve. He hated makeup and big jewelry.

Alex made her way cautiously down the stairs. The house was quiet. Her mom was in the garage, working on her pottery. She'd set up a mini studio on one side, their red SUV exiled to the driveway. Tommy was . . . well, she had no idea. She recalled him saying something about going to the library, or maybe it was to Whataburger. Probably Whataburger. Food always won out for Tommy.

Her stomach tightened. *Stop it,* she told herself. *You can't be nervous about going into your own kitchen.*

But she was.

She paused, listening to the low tones of Ava's and Luke's voices. She wondered if she could convince her parents that she needed a tutor too. Ava was so lucky.

Alex straightened her necklace, took a deep breath, and entered the kitchen.

Luke Grabowski sat next to her sister at the round table. A science textbook lay open between them. Luke reached across Ava and pointed to a graph, explaining the rate of photosynthesis.

Alex tried not to stare at him, but it was impossible. His pale-blue eyes reminded her of the sky in July. His sandy hair curled adorably near his ears, and when he smiled, he had a dimple in his right cheek. And he was smart. That was why Tommy had suggested having him tutor Ava, who always struggled with homework. Luke was in high school, like Tommy.

When Alex had first met her twin's tutor, she'd gone speechless. Since then, she couldn't stop thinking about him. If anyone could take her mind off cute Corey, it was even-cuter Luke.

Ava lifted her head, noticing Alex. She raised her eyebrows at her sister's outfit and makeup.

"Where are you going?"

"Nowhere," Alex said breezily. "Just studying."

"Oh, really," Ava said knowingly. Ava wore a faded sweatshirt, shorts, and flip-flops. Almost the same outfit Alex had on before Luke arrived.

"So photosynthesis uses sunlight to convert water and carbon dioxide into what?" Luke asked.

Alex hovered by the counter, hoping he would look up and notice her. She pretended to inspect the apples in the fruit bowl.

"Come on, we went over this," he encouraged Ava.

"Yeah, I know." Ava stalled, biting her lip. "How about a hint?"

"Energy and—?" Luke said.

Ava stared at the refrigerator door as if she'd find the answer written there.

Come on, Ave, Alex thought. *The answer's so easy.*

Ava scrunched her forehead.

"Sugar," Alex blurted out. She couldn't hold back.

"Correct!" Luke caught her eye and grinned. Alex smiled back. She felt special, and then she felt absurd because she'd just completed that worksheet yesterday.

"I knew that." Ava groaned.

"Ava sometimes has problems focusing," Alex explained to Luke.

"Alex!" Ava cried.

"Sorry, Ave." She was just trying to be helpful. Tommy had mentioned that Luke had a younger brother who also had difficulties in school, and she didn't want him to think Ava wasn't smart. They were a smart family. Luke should know that.

"Why are you here, Al? Do you need something?" Ava asked pointedly.

"I was *parched*," Alex said, using one of her vocabulary words. She pulled a glass from the cabinet. She lifted the handle on the sink faucet gracefully, aware that they were both watching her, and let the water run.

"Your mind is definitely not on green plants today, Ava," Luke said, not acknowledging Alex's advanced vocabulary. "I know you know this and more. What's up?"

Alex's heart turned to mush. He truly cared why Ava wasn't getting this science stuff. How amazing was he?

"We lost the game today. I can't stop thinking about it." Ava twirled her pencil angrily. "I hate losing."

"Me too," Luke agreed.

"You did have that awesome kick," Alex reminded her, eager to stay in the conversation.

"Yeah?" Luke asked. "How long?"

"Thirty-two yards," Ava said. "We tied up the score at the half with my kick, and then we fell apart."

"That stinks," Luke agreed, interested in the game. He'd played football when he was younger, but he hadn't gone out for the high school team. "What happened?"

"The wide receiver, I think that's his position, botched a bunch of plays," Alex explained, moving toward Luke. "His rhythm was totally off. Talk about a focus problem—"

"Al, what's with your water?" Ava interrupted.

"I'm waiting for it to get cold." Alex waved off her twin's question. "I felt the wide receiver didn't have enough flash-and-dash," she started to explain to Luke. She honestly had no idea if the guy was doing the right thing on the field or not, but she hoped the flash-and-dash phrase made her sound as if she did.

"It's *already* cold," Ava said. "You shouldn't keep the water running like that."

Alex fumed as she returned to the sink, filled her glass, and shut off the tap. She so wanted to keep talking with Luke. About anything—even football.

"So back to photosynthesis." Luke pointed to the textbook. "Leaves contain a natural chemical called what?"

"I know this one. Chlorophyll," Ava said.

"Awesome!" Luke reached up his hand, and Ava slapped him a high five.

Alex wished he'd give her a high five too. She stood awkwardly near the sink as they reviewed the stages of photosynthesis. She looked down at her cute outfit. Luke hadn't said anything. He seemed more interested in plants and sunlight than in her. She tried to think of something exciting to say. Something a high school girl would say.

She couldn't think of anything.

She placed the full glass of water on the counter and headed back upstairs. She needed a tutor of her own. Not for science or math or English. She needed someone to teach her how to get an older boy to notice her.

"What's the problem?" Alex cried, bursting into Ms. Palmer's classroom after school on Monday.

"No idea." Chloe Klein sat on a desk, swinging her legs back and forth. Her socks had the same polka-dot pattern as the fabric headband that held back her straight, honey-brown hair.

"Mystery to me." Johnny Morton bit into an apple and held up a piece of pale-blue paper. "You get this too?"

"The same." Alex read her note from Ms. Palmer aloud. "'Emergency student council meeting after school in my room for the three presidents only. Big decision to be made.'"

"I got the same one," Chloe said. "Ooh, sounds like a scandal. I wonder what happened."

"No scandal. Nothing so dramatic," Ms. Palmer assured them, hurrying into the room. "Actually, that's not true. It *is* dramatic."

"I love drama." Chloe clapped her hands together. "Spill, please!"

"Should I shut the door?" Alex asked.

"Not yet," Ms. Palmer said, as a tall woman in a deep-purple dress and two students Alex didn't recognize filed in. "Okay, now."

With the door closed, they all pulled the desks into a small circle.

Mrs. Palmer introduced the woman. "This is Mrs. Martinique. She teaches eighth-grade English and is the drama club adviser. She brought two students from the club. Eighth graders, right?"

"Yes. This is Spencer Mills and Nicole Patel. Thank you for coming today." Mrs. Martinique looked at each of the three presidents as she spoke. "It means a lot to us. I will let Spencer and Nicole tell you of our plight." She spoke in a calm, measured tone, but Alex noticed her twisting her fingers together in her lap. Her knuckles grew white.

Alex's phone buzzed. She glanced down. It was a text from Ava. She typed back a quick response.

Over the top of her half-glasses, Ms. Palmer shot her a disapproving look.

"Sorry." Alex switched the tone to silent.

Spencer stood. "The drama club is mounting the musical *The Wizard of Oz* next month. We're doing the whole show." With this, he dramatically flung his arms wide. "The performances in rehearsal have been ah-mazing, if I may say so."

"It's true." Chloe nodded vigorously. "I'm in the show. I'm just an unnamed Munchkin, although privately I call myself Twinkle Toes, because I get to dance. Isn't that cute? Spencer is a big deal. He's the Scarecrow."

Spencer broke into a spontaneous dance. He wiggled and shuffled his gangly arms and legs, then dropped dramatically to the floor, as if his limbs were truly made of straw.

Alex clapped loudly. She couldn't help herself. "You're so good!"

Spencer bowed deeply. "Thank you. I'm much better when I sing, too."

"But you may never see that," Nicole interjected gravely. Her thick, dark eyebrows knit together as she spoke. "Without your help, all our hard work will be for nothing, and the show will never go on."

"You need *our* help?" Alex asked. She'd never been in a musical before. Tommy was the only one who could sing. He said that she and Ava sang like cats with bad colds.

"Yes," Nicole went on. "The drama club stores our costumes, sets, and props in the school's basement. We have years and years of amazing costumes down there. This summer the pipes leaked. Plumbers fixed them before school started, but when we went down this weekend to pull out what we needed for the show, everything was covered with mold."

"Can't you just wash that off?" Johnny asked. He gnawed on his apple core.

"No," Nicole answered. "Everything is ruined!"

"Everything?" Alex asked.

"Everything," Mrs. Martinique confirmed. "All the costumes and props had to be tossed. We have nothing to use for the yellow brick road or

Oz. We have no ruby slippers and good or bad witches' costumes."

"Without costumes and sets, we will have to cancel the musical," Nicole said quietly. "We don't have enough money to buy what we need. And there's nothing left in the school's activity budget for us. Not a big surprise, but drama club doesn't rank very high around here."

"That's horrible," Alex said. "I love *The Wizard of Oz*. My sister and I used to watch it all the time when we were little and then click our heels to go home. Of course, we already were home, but still . . ."

"We came here to ask for your help," Spencer said. "We need money to replace what we lost, so little kids in Ashland can see the show and click their heels just like you, and so all the performers who have been working so hard can do what they love."

"But we don't have any money either, do we?" Johnny asked Ms. Palmer.

"Actually, technically, we do." She pulled off her half-glasses and let them dangle on the beaded chain around her neck. "We haven't paid for the new scoreboard yet. It's scheduled to be delivered Thursday, but that can be changed. That money is still there."

"Whoa! You want to back out of getting the scoreboard?" Johnny cried.

"I didn't say that. All I wanted to do was bring the different options to the table." Ms. Palmer turned to Mrs. Martinique. "If you don't mind, we should discuss this privately."

"Of course." The drama adviser stood, and Spencer and Nicole did too. "I thank you for considering our predicament."

"Please use your brain and your heart and have the courage to make the choice that's best for the school," Spencer said in his Scarecrow voice, as they left the room. "The *whole* school."

Once they were alone, Chloe spoke first. "There's already a scoreboard on the field. The drama club is in serious need."

"We can't do that," Johnny protested. "We made a promise to the football team and the students. We promised the scoreboard. We can't change our minds."

"We'll get them their scoreboard next year. The show is an emergency!" Chloe cried.

"You're just saying that because you're in it.

You're not thinking of the good of the whole school," Johnny countered.

"Neither are you," Chloe said. "All you think about is sports, sports, sports."

"Wake up," Johnny said. "That's what just about every kid here thinks about. If they're not playing the game, they're cheerleading or dancing or marching with the band or watching from the stands. The scoreboard makes the most sense."

"Alex," Ms. Palmer said, raising her hand to silence Johnny and Chloe. "You've been awfully quiet. Let's hear your thoughts."

"I haven't formulated an opinion yet," Alex admitted. "I see both sides: Everyone is expecting the scoreboard, and I think promises should be kept. But I feel so badly for the drama kids. It would be horrible if they couldn't do the show. And the show is important to the school too. What do you think, Ms. P?"

"It's a tough one," she agreed. "But it's a student council choice. I will support whatever you decide, but I can't make the choice for you."

"I vote we stick with our original plan," Johnny said firmly.

"I vote we delay the scoreboard and help the drama club," Chloe said.

They both looked to Alex. She squirmed uncomfortably. They were each so sure. She wished there were enough money to do both.

"Come on, Alex. I know you're going for the scoreboard, right?" Johnny urged. "Football is in your blood. You have to vote like a Sackett."

Alex stiffened. How dare he! She'd hadn't once thought of her dad or even Ava during this whole conversation. All she wanted was to do what the students had elected her to do. To make the best choices for the school.

Why did it always come back to football? Her whole life was defined by a sport she didn't even play. She thought of her mother and the beautiful pottery she made out in the garage. Mrs. Sackett was so creative and artistic, yet when anyone thought of their family, they automatically thought football.

We're more than football, she thought.

"I vote to give the money to the drama club," Alex announced. As she said it, she knew she'd made the right choice. "My dad loves football, but he always taught me to help those in need. The drama club needs us. The football team doesn't *need* a new scoreboard, at least not in the same way. We'll raise more money to get the scoreboard next year."

Chloe grinned. Johnny angrily tossed his apple core toward the wastebasket. They all listened as it plunked into the metal can.

"I will contact the company and halt the delivery of the scoreboard," Ms. Palmer said. "An announcement will have to be made over the loudspeaker tomorrow, informing the student body of the decision and explaining our rationale. Johnny?"

"I am not doing that." Johnny crossed his arms over his chest. "No way."

"I can do it," Chloe offered. "I want to do commercials someday. It will be good practice."

"Let's keep this quiet until tomorrow," Ms. Palmer suggested. "I need to clear everything with the administration."

"No problem. I'm not telling anyone about this," Johnny said.

"Johnny, we need to be unified on this," Alex reminded him. "You can't be—"

Johnny sighed. "I'm not going to do or say anything. It's your show."

"Actually, it's a show for the whole school,

and we saved it. That's *really* cool," Alex said. "Can we tell Spencer and Nicole? I'm sure I hear them waiting outside the door."

"Go for it," Mrs. Palmer said.

As she opened the door, Alex felt like the great and powerful Oz, granting wishes.

"Hey, guys, wait up!" Ava pushed her locker door shut. Corey's red hair was easy to spot at a distance. She hurried to catch up with him and Xander on their way to the locker room after school.

"Chocolate or fruit?" Corey asked when she reached them. "Which side are you on?"

"Chocolate, for sure," Ava said, adjusting her backpack on her left shoulder. "Why are we taking sides?"

"Energy bars," Xander explained. "O'Sullivan here is trying to convince me that if I go with the fruit bar, I'll run faster."

"It's a proven fact," Corey said. "Chocolate hypes you up, but then you crash. It's a sugar bomb."

"I never crash, man." Xander jogged in place. "I just keep going and going."

"Yeah, I saw how you kept going on Saturday, right past that ginormous tackle when you were supposed to be guarding me. That guy snuck by and pummeled me!" Corey's blue eyes glinted with fun as he pushed his hands together in prayer. "I beg you to go with the fruit. For my safety."

Xander turned serious for a moment. "That was bad. I'm on it this week." He grinned. "Going to double up on my chocolate, and—*boom!*—no one will get to you!"

Ava laughed. Xander was at least two heads taller than she was, and his shoulders had filled out already, unlike many boys on the team. He had a great kick and often played punter, but his strength made him a tough guard on their offensive line. As quarterback, Corey relied on him.

They slowed as they reached the two locker-room doors. Ava eyed the tarnished metal signs on each. BOYS. GIRLS. Side by side but worlds apart. Ava wondered what went on in the boys' locker room. Did she miss major team bonding in the ten minutes it took her to pull on her heavy pads and practice jersey?

"We're going to turn it around this week," Ava said, pausing as two blond volleyball players pushed the GIRLS door open. "The pieces will come together at practice."

"You planning on being there?" Xander asked.

"Of course." A spark of anger ignited in her stomach. When would these boys start taking her seriously? She was committed to the team.

"Well then, it's going to be fumble central," he remarked.

"What does that mean?" Ava jumped to the defensive. "I can catch Corey's passes!"

"We're not talking about you," Corey said. "It's Owen. With you nearby, he can't keep his eyes on the ball."

"What do I have to do with him not catching?" Ava was sick of being blamed. "It's not like I'm pulling the ball away from him."

"Clueless much?" Xander shook his head. "Wake up, Sackett. You've messed up his focus. Our best receiver is too busy looking at you."

"Why would he be looking at me? That makes no sense," Ava sputtered.

"Because he likes you," Xander said simply.

"Owen likes you," Corey agreed. "He likes you *a lot*."

CHAPTER FOUR

What do those idiots know? Ava asked herself as she changed in the girls' locker room. She desperately wished Alex was here to analyze that weird conversation. Alex knew so much more about the strange things boys said.

WHERE ARE YOU? she texted her twin.

INTENSE COUNCIL MTG!!! Alex responded.

Ava knew how wrapped up in student government her sister got. She'd have to wait to talk with Alex at home. *Just play your game.* She repeated her dad's advice as she stepped into the afternoon sunshine and joined the line of players for warm-ups. *Corey and Xander were probably trying to rile me up.*

Together the team touched their toes and lunged to the sides. After high-knee jogging and hurdle stretches, they dropped for thirty push-ups and a series of sit-ups. Ava put every ounce of energy into stretching and loosening her muscles. Only when they moved on to sprints did she finally dare to look Owen's way.

He was staring at her.

She upped her speed and glanced back at him once more. His eyes held a glassy, dreamy look while he watched her run.

Yikes! Ava wanted to race right off the field.

She finished her turn and bent over to catch her breath, her hands resting on her thighs. She wondered what to do. Then she noticed Coach Kenerson watching Owen . . . watching her.

He frowned, as late to the party as she was, suddenly realizing where Owen's attention had been all week. His head turned from Owen to her and back again, silently calculating what to do.

Ava held her breath. She hoped he wouldn't embarrass Owen in front of the team.

He blew his whistle. "Sackett, head to the far end with Coach MacDonald to work on kicking drills. Everyone else with me and Coach D'Annolfo."

"Just me?" Ava asked. Usually all the kids who played kicker—she, Xander, and Bryce Hobson—practiced together.

"Yes," Coach K grunted, then turned his back.

Ava jogged down to the goalpost where Coach MacDonald waited. She was being banished, she realized. Kept apart from the team, and specifically from Owen. Out of his sight.

It wasn't fair, she knew, but she could deal with it. Besides, having a private session was helpful. Ava tried her hardest to improve her kicks. More loft. More distance. Better follow-through. The team's voices floated her way between kicks.

"You're hitting the ball cleanly. Let's try a quality kick." Coach MacDonald held the ball at the thirty yard line.

At the other end of the field, Coach K barked at the team to run a sidelines-catching drill.

Ava focused on her own kick, although she could clearly hear Corey shouting commands. She took three steps away, then approached at game speed. Her eyes never left Coach MacDonald's fingers, as she let her shoulders lead her through the ball. Her foot connected and the ball soared gracefully between the two goalposts.

A chorus of groans rose up from the other end of the field. Ava twisted in time to see Owen fumble Corey's pass. He stood, gazing instead at her field goal.

"Rooney!" Coach K did not mask his anger. "Sprints on the bleachers. Now!"

"How many?" Owen asked, his voice barely audible to Ava.

"As many as it takes for you to focus on the ball in front of you! Think about that while you run!" Coach K sputtered.

With a sinking sensation, Ava realized Owen once again had messed up because of her. Even all the way down the field, his attention had been on her kick.

"There goes this Saturday's game, too," Coach MacDonald muttered softly.

Owen's cleats clattered as he ascended the metal bleachers. Several players turned toward Ava. Were they giving her dirty looks? She couldn't be sure from so far away.

She didn't know what to think. She'd never had a boy so openly interested in her. It was kind of flattering, even though she didn't like him in that way. Or at least it would be flattering, if he could catch the ball at the same time.

Now it was just embarrassing.

She desperately needed to talk to Alex. She had to put a stop to this—or soon Coach K and the whole team would blame her.

After practice ended, Ava hurried into the locker room, for once glad to be away from the team. She peeled off her jersey and put on the outfit she'd worn to school. Jeans, a gray Boston Celtics T-shirt, and her green high-top Converses. Her T-shirts often featured a sports team, although she did have some solid ones. Alex called those her "feeble attempt at fashion." Ava didn't care. Comfort was key. Listening in class was tricky enough without wearing a little skirt or lace-trimmed tank like Alex did.

Glancing at the clock on the wall, Ava grabbed her backpack and raced out the door. The sports late bus left promptly at five p.m. Missing it meant calling her mom for a ride, or walking a few miles, and she didn't want to do either. Her mom was crunched this week with all her new orders, and Ava was tired.

"Hey!"

"Oh, hey!" Ava nearly collided with Owen outside the girls' locker room.

"That was a really great kick," he said quickly.

His cheeks were rosy from the sprints up and down the bleachers.

"Uh, thanks." Ava scanned the empty hallway. Everyone else must have run for the bus.

"Listen, uh . . . I was wondering . . ." Owen paused and stared at his feet. Ava smelled that musky, chocolate-tinged deodorant all the boys sprayed over themselves.

An awkward silence hung over them. Ava debated saying something about the practice, about him staring at her, but she couldn't piece together any words. Maybe she should bring up Kylie or that fantasy site they were on.

"Are you walking home?" Owen finally blurted out. His eyes stayed trained on his sneakers.

"No, I usually take the late bus. I live pretty far. Why?" she asked.

"Oh, yeah, well, I walk and I—I—I wanted to, well, uh . . . ," he stammered. The rosiness from his cheeks crept down his neck.

A loud buzz blared over the loudspeakers. The final call for the bus.

Ava gulped. "Listen, I really need to—"

"I just wanted . . . I mean, if it's okay . . . I thought—"

"Sorry, but I have to go." Ava took off down

the hall at top speed. "Sorry!" she called again over her shoulder.

Ava had to make the bus—she couldn't wait any longer for him to get out whatever he was trying to say. And truthfully, a big part of her didn't want to hear it. From all his stuttering and blushing, she was now sure Owen liked her.

She had no idea what to do about that.

"What's for dinner?" Alex asked, entering the kitchen that night. She'd gone to the library with Chloe after the meeting, and Chloe's mom had just driven her home.

Tommy's textbooks and notebook paper covered the kitchen table. "No idea," he mumbled. "Big history test tomorrow."

"I'm starving," their dad announced, coming in behind Alex.

"Me too," Ava added, trailing behind him. Her hair, wet from the shower, was wrapped in a yellow towel. "Where's Mom?"

"I'm here! I'm here!" Mrs. Sackett raced through the back door.

"Ew! What's in your hair?" Alex cried. She

guided her mom to the microwave, using the glass door as a mirror.

"Oh!" Her mom's fingers brushed the thick gray clumps. "What else? Clay."

"You look really tired." Alex noticed the dark circles under her glassy eyes. "Maybe you should—"

"What about food?" Tommy asked. "My stomach is telling me it's time to refuel."

Figures, Alex thought, looking up at the clock. Her brother's stomach was better than an alarm. The family tried to eat together at six o'clock every night.

And now it was ten minutes after six.

"Right, dinner," their mom said, as if this were a surprising idea. She opened the refrigerator and studied the contents.

Alex peered around her shoulder. Pretty slim pickings. Unless they were having a meal of condiments, cheese, and a wrinkled red pepper.

"There must be something in the freezer." Her mom pulled open the bottom drawer.

"Everything's frozen," Alex said. Her mom usually had casseroles or stews ready for dinner, but she'd been at her potter's wheel all weekend. They'd barely seen her.

"Michael, I wish you had gone to the market this weekend," Mrs. Sackett said, eyeing her husband.

"It's football season, Laur, you know that," he replied.

"The game was *Friday* night," her mother pointed out.

"And on Saturday I started preparing for this week's game. This is a big one coming up. The Cleary Titans. Besides, you didn't tell me to go to the market," he protested.

"I need to tell you? You could figure it out too."

"You can't blame me. Maybe you're in over your head with these orders—"

"I'm not in over my head!" her mom shot back. "I've got it all covered."

"Actually, I think it's covered you. The pottery, that is," Tommy joked.

Besides her hair, Mrs. Sackett had streaks of clay on her bare arms and shirt.

Alex tried to stifle her giggles. Ava laughed and their mom grinned, pausing to look down at herself.

Alex was glad Tommy had defused the tension. Her parents had rarely snapped at each other back in Massachusetts, but the move to

Texas had been hard. Her dad was under a lot of pressure to produce a winning team. Her mom had left behind her friends and job and now was starting a new business. A few weeks ago, the first time their mom was swamped with work, they had spent a lot of time bickering, but then Alex and Ava helped Coach surprise Mrs. Sackett with a special anniversary dinner, and things seemed to get better. Alex vowed to try to help keep her parents happy this time too.

"I'm craving pizza. Anyone else?" Alex hurried to the desk and opened the top drawer, where they kept the take-out menus. "Sal's Pizzeria delivers. Good?"

Her parents both nodded.

"Extra sausage on mine," Tommy said. "Or meatballs."

Alex grimaced. "You're such a carnivore!"

"Grr! I'm an Ashland Tiger," he growled with a mischievous grin.

Alex rolled her eyes. She called in their order for two pizzas and made sure the second one had no meat. She'd been a vegetarian for several months now.

Once the steaming pizzas arrived and the table had been set, Alex could see her mom relax. She told them about the new pots she'd created. Her dad worried over the weather report. It looked like heavy rain was coming later in the week. He hated having his team play in the mud.

"Enough football," their mom chided. "Tell me something good that happened today at school." She liked to ask variations on this question. Some days she asked for something funny that happened at school. Or something strange. Even something bad.

"The student council did something *colossally* good," Alex said proudly. She told them about the drama club decision.

"Wait! We're not getting the new scoreboard?" Ava asked mid-bite.

"Not this year," Alex explained. "The drama club's need is bigger."

"That's not fair," Ava protested.

Coach nodded. "You did make a commitment, Al. You gave your word."

Alex was surprised. "But you always taught us to help those in need. Look out for the underdog."

"True, but I also believe you shouldn't duck out on a promise," he said. "That scoreboard is a big deal to the community."

"So is the school musical," her mom said, coming to her defense. "Schools should promote the arts. The arts should play as significant a role as sports do in students' lives."

"But everyone in Ashland would rather have a scoreboard than a school show," Ava remarked.

"Not everyone," Alex shot back. "I can't believe you, Ave. I thought you were better than all those jocks. Not so single-minded."

"I'm not that way, and you know it," Ava said, sounding hurt. "I love *The Wizard of Oz*, but I just don't agree with your decision. I think a lot of other kids will disagree too."

"You're overreacting," Alex scoffed. "Kids will be fine with waiting for the scoreboard in order to save the show. It's not a big deal."

"Not a big deal?" Tommy snorted. "The whole town shuts down when the lights go up on Friday nights."

Alex sighed. The football players in her family didn't get it. They were imagining a problem where there wasn't one. "Everything's going to be fine," she assured them.

Tommy wagged his finger at her. "We're not in Massachusetts anymore, Dorothy."

CHAPTER FIVE

Alex finished her math problems in record time that night, moving on to plow through her science lab report. Across the kitchen table, Ava chewed the eraser on her pencil and stared at the ceiling.

How can we do our homework so differently? Alex wondered. *We look exactly alike. We came from the same parents and entered the world at the same time.* Technically Alex showed up twelve minutes before Ava. "Alex is always first out the door," her mom liked to joke.

Yet Ava had barely finished half her math problems. She stared distractedly around the room between each one, while Alex pushed through, as if running a race. Tonight she wanted to spend time on a new room makeover website. Instructions for a do-it-yourself fabric bulletin board had caught her eye. If she could get her mom to help, she thought it didn't look too tricky.

"Ready to work?" Luke sauntered into the kitchen, surprising both of them. "Tommy let me in."

"Hi!" Alex sang, stunned by his warm smile. She quickly straightened the gray T-shirt and flannel pajama pants she'd changed into after dinner. Why hadn't anyone told her Luke was coming? She would have worn something pretty. And put on makeup. Oh no! What did her face look like? She hadn't looked in the mirror since she'd come home.

"Oops, I forgot about you," Ava admitted. "But I'm glad you're here. I'm kind of stuck."

Luke pulled out a chair, then turned to Alex. "Sorry to kick you out of your study space."

"No problem." Alex gathered her books. "I was done anyway."

"Okay, cool." He pointed to her pencil sketch on her lab report. "Awesome cell diagram."

"Really? Thanks!"

We're having our first real conversation! Alex realized.

"What are you working on now?" he asked.

"Still scien—" Alex began.

"Math," Ava answered, and Alex belatedly understood the question hadn't been for her.

"How are the problems going?" Luke had turned his full attention to Ava.

Alex felt hurt, then reminded herself that her parents were paying him to tutor Ava, not talk with her. She took her time organizing her papers.

"I can't answer a lot," Ava admitted.

Luke glanced at her worksheet. "You're not trying. I know you can do these. Something is up, right?"

"Yeah," Ava admitted slowly.

Alex gaped at Luke. How did he know? She was usually the first to sense when something bothered Ava.

"Football trouble," Ava explained.

"You should talk to Daddy or Tommy," Alex advised. "They'll help."

"It's not *that* kind of football trouble." Ava rapidly twirled her chewed-up pencil. "It's boy football trouble." The story of Owen spilled out.

Ava squeezed her eyes shut as she finished. "Now the whole team is angry. They blame me."

"How can they blame you? You didn't do anything," Alex said. "You never asked him to like you."

"Exactly!" Ava cried.

"It doesn't matter," Luke interjected. "To a guy, it's very black and white. Owen's skills are tanking, and he's flipped out over you; therefore, other guys say you're the cause. No gray area there."

"That's ridiculous!" Alex said. "Maybe I could talk to them."

"Could you?" Ava sounded relieved.

"No," Luke said. "Ava, you need to handle this on your own. Be proactive and stop it cold before this poor guy gets more lovesick and lousier on the field."

"Stop what?" Ava asked. "What am I supposed to stop?"

"Stop him from liking you," Luke said simply.

"Oh, yeah, like that's easy," Ava scoffed.

"Find out all the things this Owen kid dislikes in a girl. The things that bother or annoy him." Luke grinned. "Then do them. All of them!"

"I like the way you think!" Alex cried,

impressed with his take-charge attitude. "Owen will want nothing to do with you, Ave."

A slow smile spread across Ava's face. "I could do that."

Alex agreed. "You can fix this easily."

Alex put Mission: Owen into effect Tuesday morning when she entered school. She'd agreed to help Ava, and her first stop was her friend Emily Campbell's locker. Emily lived next door to Owen, and as far as Alex knew, they'd known each other since they were in diapers.

"Love your top!" Alex called, as she approached.

Emily gazed up and grinned. "It's cute, right? I pulled it out of Julia's closet after she left this morning. She's only worn it once. I'm so dead if she finds out, but I figure I can put it back before she gets home. The high school lets out ten minutes after us."

"Impressive! Living on the edge in the name of fashion." Alex admired the rhinestones on the hem of Emily's blue-green ombré shirt. "You're so lucky that your sister has such an awesome closet to raid. You'll have to run home fast. You live nearby, right?"

"Down the street." Emily tucked her long blond hair behind her ears, as she leaned against her locker door.

"Oh right, aren't you on the same block as Owen Rooney?" Alex asked, as if she'd just stumbled on this fact. This was going easier than she'd planned.

"Next door. You know Owen?"

"Kind of. Not really." Alex leaned closer and lowered her voice. "Can you tell me about him?"

Emily's eyes lit up. "What do you want to know?"

"Anything. Likes. Dislikes . . ." Alex's voice trailed off as Lindsey approached.

"Who are we talking about?" Lindsey dropped her canvas book bag onto the floor to rearrange her blond hair into its ponytail. Lindsey and Emily were the "three Bs": blond, beautiful, and best friends. Alex had known instantly on the first day of school that they were the popular ones, and popular was where she wanted to be. She hadn't wasted any time becoming their friends. The added bonus was that they both turned out to be really nice.

"We're talking about Owen!" Emily squealed.

"Shh!" Alex cautioned, glancing around. The halls were crowded, but kids seemed more intent on putting books in lockers and getting to homeroom than listening to them. One more high-pitched squeal from Emily would quickly change that.

"Alex wants to know what he likes in a girl," Emily confided to Lindsey.

"Really? You and Owen?" Lindsey sidled closer to Alex. She paused as if considering the match. "He seems a little quiet for you."

"He's not bad-looking," Emily put in. "And he's super nice."

"I'm not asking for me," Alex protested.

"Oh, please, like we'd ever believe that whole 'I'm asking for a friend' routine." Lindsey wrapped her arm warmly around Alex's shoulder. "You don't have to be shy with us. I like the idea of you being interested in Owen. I like it a lot!"

Alex was startled by Lindsey's reaction. Not that Alex had totally stopped liking Corey, but she'd assumed that with the two of them dating, and after she'd pretended to date and break up with Ava's best friend Charlie from back in Boston,

Lindsey no longer viewed Alex as a threat.

Maybe she'd been wrong.

"Em, tell her everything you know," Lindsey encouraged.

"Seriously," Alex said. "I'm not asking for me. It's for"—she knew Ava did not want her situation to go viral—"a girl on student council."

"Really?" Emily asked suspiciously.

"Cross my heart," Alex assured her. "I'm so not interested in him."

"Who is?" Lindsey asked.

"A sixth-grade girl who'd be mortified if I told you," Alex said. "So what's Owen's type?"

"I don't think he's ever had a girlfriend," Emily said. "He's very chill, you know? He keeps things simple. He'd go for an easygoing girl he could pal around with. He doesn't like show-off girly-girl types. Whenever I wear makeup and go to the mall, he gets on my case. He hates the smell of hair spray and, get this, lavender. He gags when I wear my lavender hand cream." She thrust her hand under Alex's nose. "I think it smells nice, don't you?"

"It's pretty," Alex agreed, making a mental list for Ava. Already she could see why Owen liked her sister. "Anything else?"

"He likes sports and, oh yeah, he hates cats. Can't stand them."

"Good to know," Alex remarked. Where could she rustle up a cat for Ava?

"I need a list like this for Greg Fowler," Emily said with a sigh.

"Isn't he a twin too?" Alex asked.

Emily nodded. "Greg is so much cuter than his brother Tim."

"I want Em to hurry and get together with Greg, and then Corey and I can go with them to the dance," Lindsey confided.

Instantly Alex saw them in her mind. Lindsey and Corey entering the dance, hand in hand, everyone turning to admire them. The perfect couple. Her insides twisted at the vision, and then the vision itself twisted. Now she stood in Lindsey's place.

Hand in hand with Corey, their fingers intertwined.

"I'm working up my nerve," Emily said, jolting Alex back to reality. "I borrowed Greg's pencil yesterday."

"What about you, Alex? Who's your dream date for the dance?" Lindsey prodded.

Your boyfriend.

Alex gulped. Yeah, right. But she had to say something.

"He's in high school," she blurted out.

"For real? Tell all!" Lindsey commanded.

"His name is Luke, and he's friends with my brother Tommy," Alex explained. "He's over at our house a lot, and we've talked a bunch."

"Just you and him? Without Tommy?" Emily asked.

"Yeah. Really deep conversations. Not like this middle school stuff, you know?" Alex didn't mention that he was Ava's tutor. She didn't think her sister wanted that private information circulating either. "He appreciates how much I care about school. And he's so insanely cute!"

"A high school boy!" Emily squealed. "Do you think you'll see him again soon?"

"He told me specifically he was coming by my house later this week," Alex said.

Emily's eyes bulged with admiration. Even Lindsey looked impressed.

"Well, got to get to class," Alex said, knowing that if she stayed any longer, she risked messing up her story. As cute as Corey was, her high school guy totally outranked a middle school quarterback.

I did not lie, she reminded herself as she walked away. She pushed down the tendril of guilt snaking through her brain. Luke *had* told her he was coming back for another tutoring session. Besides, Lindsey had asked about her dream date. Luke was the definition of a dream date.

If she couldn't go out with Corey, she might as well dream about Luke.

Ava was dying to turn around.

Eyes on the board, she reminded herself. She watched Jack find the missing angle of an obtuse triangle. He attacked the problem, writing on the board with sure, certain strokes.

I'll look back after he finishes. No, after the next problem is solved, she decided.

Ever since the beginning of math class, Ava had been twisting in her seat to catch a glimpse of Owen.

Owen watching her.

His gray-green eyes trained on her.

As if she were doing something interesting.

She didn't get it. She'd barely had time to

brush her hair and throw on a sweatshirt this morning before racing to catch the bus. He'd be better off staring at Bridget Malloy, who sat next to her. Her shiny hair was woven into an intricate French braid with turquoise ribbon expertly threaded through it. And the ribbon matched her turquoise ruffled shirt!

Ava shook her head. No, Owen should be thinking about Kylie. She hoped Alex was getting good dirt on Owen, so she could shut down this staring business. But she also needed to get him interested in Kylie. Maybe that was the trick. If she could show him how great Kylie was, he'd stop caring about *her*. Kylie was awesome. He just didn't know it yet.

She jolted when the end-of-class bell rang. She hadn't noticed the time. As all the kids pushed toward the door, she gathered the worksheets scattered haphazardly across her desk.

I have to get organized, she thought for the millionth time as she shoved the papers into her binder, not bothering to open the rings. Two worksheets fluttered to the floor, and she knelt to pick them up.

"Need help?" Owen hovered above her, looking amused.

"No, no, I'm good," she assured him, righting herself. She glanced around. They were the only two left in the classroom. Even Mrs. Vargas had fled.

Another awkward silence.

Owen watched her expectantly.

Ava wished a football would suddenly appear. If she had a football to toss with him, things would feel normal. They wouldn't have to talk if they had a football.

"Great kick yesterday," Owen said.

"Thanks," Ava replied shakily. *Why is he repeating himself? And why am I so nervous?* She never usually had problems talking to boys about sports. *And that's what this is,* she reminded herself. *We're talking about football.*

"The wind was cooperating yesterday," she went on. "I hate that dry wind you have here in Texas. Do you know what I'm talking about?"

Ava babbled on about velocity and wind speed as they headed for the door. She wondered how to transition the conversation to Kylie.

"My friend sometimes helps me with my kicks," she began, although this wasn't true.

"Look, uh," Owen broke in. "Thisisforyou.

Ithoughtyou—ImeanIhopeyou—" His words rocketed out in an enormous run-on sentence that she couldn't decipher.

Face flushed, Owen tried to continue. "Iboughtthisforyou." He thrust a small pink box with a tiny bow into her hands. Then he took off down the hall, racing away as if the opposing team had sent all their linebackers after him.

Ava watched him go in a daze. Slowly she lifted the top off the box. A delicate silver bracelet lay nestled in a fluff of white cotton. She lifted it to the light. A tiny silver football charm dangled from the bracelet's center.

She blinked rapidly. A boy had given her jewelry. *Her! Jewelry!* The concept was too unreal.

She wished she liked him back. But she didn't.

She thought of the team. Of Coach K's disapproving glare. Of Corey and Xander's frustration as Owen failed to complete pass after pass. And of Kylie's eager face.

She tucked the bracelet back into its box. She would give it back. No question about that.

She wondered what would happen next. Would returning Owen's gift make things better—or worse?

CHAPTER SIX

"Alex! I've been looking for you!"

The halo of Ms. Palmer's frizzy auburn hair rose above the crowd in the hallway.

"Alex!" Ms. Palmer's voice grew louder, and kids turned. "It's urgent!"

Uh-oh. Ms. Palmer was her English teacher, as well as the student council adviser. Alex quickly reviewed what had happened in class yesterday. Had she done something wrong? Ms. Palmer had given them a timed write on *Lord of the Flies*, but Alex thought she had done fine. She knew she had written at least a page more than the girl next to her had.

"Quick! Come with me. We'll talk and walk."

Ms. Palmer reached for Alex's shoulder and guided her down the hall at a clipped pace. "I need you to jump in."

"Where?" Alex dodged elbows and shoelaces in an effort to keep up. She gripped her brown paper bag that held the turkey sandwich her dad had made for lunch.

"Chloe went home sick. She was supposed to announce the student council's reallocation of the funds over the loudspeaker."

"When?"

"Right now." Ms. Palmer slowed in front of the office. "I need you to make the announcement. I wrote it out for you. Short and sweet. Okay?"

Ms. Palmer didn't leave her any time to decide. Before she knew it, she stood in front of the microphone. Ms. Palmer thrust a smartphone in front of her with the screen open to a paragraph.

"And now a special announcement from seventh-grade class president Alexandra Sackett," Mrs. Gusman, the school secretary, said over the loudspeaker. Alex cleared her throat and began to read from the tiny screen.

A moment later Mrs. Gusman was back on, reciting a list of after-school activities.

"Thank you," Ms. Palmer breathed. "You were great. Professional, even."

Alex thought her voice sounded good. She'd made herself speak slowly. "No problem!" She waved as she left the office.

The smells of taco sauce and nacho cheese assaulted her as she pushed through the cafeteria door. Lunch period was halfway over, and the overcooked scent of the hot lunch made her hungry. She glanced toward her usual table in the back. Shrieks of laughter, the clatter of silverware, a chant from the girls' volleyball team filled the tightly packed room. She wondered if her friends had even heard her over the roar in here.

The noise was so soft at first that she didn't register it.

Then it rose around her. A low rumbling.

Alex glanced sideways toward a table crammed with boys sitting shoulder to shoulder. Paper plates piled with taco remains littered the surface in front of them. They booed in unison.

Alex startled, frozen to the spot. *Are they booing at me?*

She checked her clothes. Everything was in place. No embarrassing stains that she could see.

No sticky notes with weird messages attached.

The booing grew loud enough for her to hear, but not loud enough to attract the teachers' attention. She recognized a few faces. Football players. Boys on Ava's team.

They kept booing.

And it was definitely meant for *her*!

Alex bolted toward Lindsey and Emily. Out of the corner of her eye, she spotted Ava across the large room, but Lindsey and Emily were closer. All she wanted was to sit with her friends and figure out what was going on.

"Hi." Alex fought to keep the strain out of her voice. She squeezed onto the bench alongside Emily and Rosa Navarro. Breathing deeply, she forced her body to relax and pulled her sandwich from her bag. Everything would be okay now.

"Hi," Emily said, the single word noticeably frosty.

"Traitor," muttered Xander, who sat across from her and next to Corey and Lindsey.

"Excuse me?" Alex asked.

"That was really harsh, Alex, what you did." Xander crossed his arms defiantly across his chest.

"What I did?" Alex's eyes darted nervously

about the table, landing on Corey. Corey's usually warm, playful smile had turned icy.

"You canceled the scoreboard," Lindsey
explained.

"That wasn't me. That was the student council," Alex defended herself.

"But aren't you on the student council?"
Xander asked.

"Yeah, aren't you our *president*?" Rosa added,
emphasizing her title and the blame that suddenly came with it.

"Yes, but—" She explained the drama club's
plight and repeated her promise to buy the
scoreboard next year. "The team can still play
this year without a new scoreboard. A touchdown is a touchdown even if you have to scratch
the score in the dirt."

"What?" Xander cried. "You want us to do
that?"

Corey echoed his outrage.

Immediately Alex realized her mistake. "I
didn't mean it like that. All I'm saying is that the
scoreboard you have still works, and whether
it's new or old, it doesn't affect how you play or
if you play. Without sets and costumes, there'd
be no musical."

"That makes no sense," Corey scoffed.

"Girls shouldn't be allowed to make decisions like this," Xander added.

"It's not a girl thing. *I* would have chosen the scoreboard," Rosa insisted, tearing into a bag of chips. She offered some to Emily and Lindsey.

"It wasn't just me!" Alex repeated. She chewed her sandwich slowly. The turkey felt dry against her throat.

For a moment, no one said anything. Then Lindsey began comparing flavors at a new frozen yogurt place. Everyone chimed in, but only Emily bothered to ask Alex her favorite.

Suddenly she wasn't hungry. "I'm going to toss this," she announced, rewrapping her sandwich. She headed across the room toward the one person who would always be on her side.

"Ave, I don't get it," Alex said, as she plopped down next to her twin.

"Get what?" Kylie leaned forward. She sat across from Ava.

"I'm guessing the football players and the cheerleaders aren't skipping down the yellow brick road after your big announcement?" Ava said.

"More like they're about to drop a house on me!"

"Sorry," Kylie said, shaking her head. "That's rough."

"And those guys"—Alex raised her chin in the direction of the boys—"were booing me! Can you believe it?"

"I told you so." Ava sighed.

Alex tilted her head. "What's that mean?"

"It means I feel bad, Al, that they're being mean, but you made the wrong choice," Ava said. "I warned you it would be a big deal."

Hot tears pricked the corners of Alex's eyes, but she blinked them back. It hurt that Ava wasn't on her side. "It wasn't only my choice! Why doesn't anybody get that?"

"Because you made the announcement," Kylie explained. "You're now the face—or the voice—behind the news. Personally, I support you and the drama kids. It's always all about football here in Ashland." She stood and reached for Alex's paper bag. "Want me to grab that?"

Alex nodded and watched Kylie walk off to toss the trash.

"Don't be sad," Ava said quietly, placing her hand on Alex's. "They'll come around. They still all like you."

"It doesn't feel that way." Alex gave her sister

a small smile. Ava knew her better than anyone. "Will you talk to Corey and Xander for me at practice?"

"I'll try. But I also have a big Owen thing to deal with at practice today."

"Nothing is bigger than this right now." Alex wondered how she hadn't predicted her friends' reactions. She'd stood up in the emergency class president meeting for what she believed was right, and she still thought she'd made the right choice, but she also needed her friends.

Maybe more than she needed the school musical.

Or a scoreboard.

She'd thought getting elected was the hard part. Who knew being on student council was going to be so tricky?

"Want to bet my problem is bigger than yours?" Ava reached into the pocket of her zip-up sweatshirt and slipped out a small box. "Check out what you-know-who just gave me."

"Oh, wow!" Alex lifted the silver bracelet from the box, momentarily speechless.

"Pretty!" Kylie cried, as she slid back into her seat. "I didn't think you wore jewelry, Ave."

"I don't." Ava snatched the bracelet and

tucked it and the box out of sight.

"Is it a sister gift?" Kylie asked. "How do I get in on this twin-giving thing?"

"It's not from me," Alex admitted, and felt Ava kick her lightly under the table. She bumped her sister's shoulder with a laugh. "Maybe another time, Ave."

"Al—" Ava started.

Alex leaned toward Kylie. "It's from Ava's admirer."

"Admirer?" Kylie wiggled her eyebrows. "Why don't I know this? Who?"

"Owen Rooney!" Alex whispered.

The moment she'd said his name, she sensed she'd done something wrong. Ava stiffened beside her, while Kylie's face crumpled.

"How—how could you do this to me?" Kylie sputtered at Ava.

"It's not what it looks like. I didn't do any-thing. I promise," Ava said.

"Then why is he giving you jewelry?" Kylie's eyes clouded with betrayal. "I told you how I felt about him. I trusted you."

Uh-oh, Alex thought. *Does Kylie like Owen?* Why hadn't Ava told her? She never would have opened her big mouth.

"I'm not interested in Owen. You have to believe me," Ava pleaded.

"Then why did he give you that bracelet?" Kylie asked.

"I don't know," Ava said.

"Did you ever talk to him about me?" Kylie asked.

Alex watched Ava's face fall. "Not yet. It's been really strange at practice. But I am going to—"

"I can see how strange it's been." Kylie stood as the bell rang and walked to the door without saying good-bye.

"I feel horrible," Ava wailed. "I didn't want to hurt her. This is all my fault. I'm messing everything up."

"No, you're not. Owen is," Alex insisted, squeezing her sister's hand. "But I know how to fix it. By tomorrow, he'll be over you."

"What about Kylie?"

"Let her cool down, then talk to her. She'll come around," Alex assured her. "Just like you told me Lindsey and Emily will."

Ava considered this. "And your plan is good?"

"Really good," Alex promised.

CHAPTER SEVEN

I hate this, Ava thought. *I really hate this.*

But for the plan to work, she had to keep moving. Keep smiling. Keep tossing her hair.

She was so not a girl who tossed her hair!

Yet here she was, Wednesday morning in the school hallway, tossing away. And everyone was watching her.

Deep breath.

She heard the whispers. And not just from the boys. The girls were staring too. A cell phone camera clicked, and she cringed. In seconds, everyone in the school would have an eyeful of her.

In her new outfit. The new Ava.

Leopard-print jeans, black sequined tank, and black heeled booties. Big silver hoop earrings and a stack of bangle bracelets jangling on her wrist. Glitter plum lip gloss and thick brown eyeliner.

She'd undergone an extreme makeover, courtesy of Alex.

"I look like a little kid playing dress-up," she'd complained to Alex early that morning, as her twin carefully applied the eyeliner.

"You look great!" Alex exclaimed. "A bit much, maybe, but plenty of girls get this dressed up for school. You'll be one of them today."

Now, with the shellacked gloss weighing on her lips and the booties pinching her toes with each wobbly step, she wondered why any girl would dress like this. She debated ducking into the locker room and changing into her practice jersey and cleats. That would be heaven.

No, she told herself. She was a team player, and she was doing this for the team. And for Kylie, too.

She'd spent a lot of time last night feeling guilty and sorry for herself. Then she'd realized that everything was happening around her. It was as if she were upset about not scoring a touchdown when she stood frozen in the middle of the field while the ball was run and passed around her.

"You've got to be part of the action," her dad always coached.

Today she was following his advice.

If Owen can suddenly decide he likes me, then I can make him unlike me, she'd decided. She wouldn't be mean. She'd turn herself into the kind of girl he didn't like and let him do the rest.

She forced herself not to look his way when she entered math class. With a confidence she never knew she had, she strutted across the room. Thankfully, Mrs. Vargas was facing the board, writing out problems.

"Holy moly, Sackett!" Jack cried.

"Hi there, Jack!" she called, her voice purposely high. She wiggled her fingers in a wave and giggled. So very unlike her. She was not a giggly girl.

Waves of confusion rolled across Jack's face. He looked like he was trying to decide whether this was a joke or she'd truly crossed to the dark side.

Ava felt bad. She wished she could have clued Jack in, but Alex had told her she couldn't risk someone spilling to Owen. She edged away from him, afraid she'd lose her nerve, and stopped at Bridget Malloy's desk.

Bridget was one of the girls who dressed up every day in skirts and sparkly shoes. A force field of perfume surrounded her. Ava barely knew Bridget, but as luck would have it, they'd been paired up yesterday in social studies for a group project—it was the perfect excuse.

With a quick glance toward Owen—he was watching—she greeted Bridget loudly, as if they were long-lost best buds, and asked about the project.

If Bridget was surprised by her sudden transformation, she rolled with it. "I love your outfit! That top is to die for! Where did you get it?" she squealed.

"The mall," Ava confided loudly enough for Owen to overhear. "I love, love, love the mall, don't you? It's my favorite place ever."

"I know, right?" Bridget grinned. "I could live at Spruce. Did you see the pink dress on the mannequin in front?"

"So cute!" Ava forced herself to giggle. "And tucked in the back was a shirt with the most adorable pink rhinestone kitty on it."

"Really? I missed that." Bridget actually looked concerned. "Do you like cats?"

"Like them? I'm *crazy* for cats. For my birthday this year, I'm getting three kittens!" Ava exclaimed.

"Three?" Bridget puckered her glossed lips in an O of surprise.

"I'm such a cat person," Ava said. Out of the corner of her eye, she detected Owen grimacing, and that fueled her confidence. "Do you know what I'm going to name them? Larkin, Louie, and Linus!"

"After Three Amigos? You like them too?"

Three Amigos was a silly teen boy band. Ava hated their high-pitched warbling. The three singers had floppy hair and chiseled good looks that all the boys on the team ridiculed.

"I thought you were one of those sporty girls. You seem so different today. What happened?" Bridget asked.

Ava felt Owen, Jack, and the rest of the class lean in to hear her answer. She giggled and waved her hand. "I like sports, but this is the real me. I was just afraid that they wouldn't take me on the team if I dressed pretty like this. The whole jersey-and-jeans thing was a costume. Did

I fool you?" She giggled again for good measure. She hoped she wasn't overdoing it.

"Totally!" Bridget cried.

As Ava slid into her seat and Mrs. Vargas started class, she allowed herself to turn in Owen's direction.

He wrinkled his forehead, looking perplexed.

Ava crossed her fingers. Had her performance worked?

Alex tried to add the line of numbers in her head, but she kept messing up. Usually math class was a breeze for her. She hated that she couldn't concentrate today.

While Ava had entered the school to a flurry of amused gasps, Alex's own reception had been harsh. Boys openly glared at her. People gave her the silent treatment. A few weeks ago, she'd ridden her wave of popularity to be elected president. Now she was being frozen out.

All because of a scoreboard.

Not everyone was unkind. The drama kids loved her. Probably the art and music kids too. But she'd suddenly realized that those kids weren't her friends. At least, not yet. The first friends she'd made in Ashland were the football players, the cheerleaders, and the halftime dancers.

And then Andy Baker came up to her before math class and, in front of Corey, Lindsey, and Emily, accused her of being "anti-football."

"Me? You think I'm anti-football?" she cried.

"All the other towns around us have high-tech boards, but because of you, we don't." Andy crossed his beefy arms. "So, yeah, I'm calling you anti-football."

The idea was so ridiculous that Alex thought she might laugh. She was a Sackett.

Instead she countered, "It was not *me*. The student council presidents made the decision."

"Ignore Andy," Emily said, as they took their seats. "He's such a hothead."

"He's not the only one."

"Yeah, a lot of the guys are going to the principal. They want her to overturn your—I mean, the student council's decision," Emily informed her.

"Seriously?" Alex wondered if this would work.

"That's what I've heard. Logan Medina is leading the charge. You know what else he's doing?"

Alex could only imagine. Logan had been her competition running for seventh-grade president. He played football and was crazy popular with the athletic kids. Losing to her had been a shock—one he hadn't taken all that well.

"He's been saying that he would have been a better choice than you," Emily confided.

"Girls!" Ms. Kerry, their math teacher, called. "No more chatting. Start solving the problem on the board."

What if Logan found a way to unseat her as president? Alex's stomach tightened at the thought.

Everything was spiraling out of control. She couldn't just sit here.

She had planned to meet up with Ava to hear about Owen, but as soon as class finished, she bolted to the West wing. Ava would have to wait. She had to see Ms. Palmer now, even if it meant being late to French.

Ms. Palmer stood in the hall outside her classroom door. "What's wrong?"

Alex told her about the football players going to the principal.

"Nonsense. The administration is behind the

decision one hundred percent," Ms. Palmer told her. "It's a fait accompli. Do you know what that means in French? A done deal."

"That doesn't change that they all hate me," Alex said. "They called me anti-football!"

The bell rang and the stragglers filed into the classroom, but Ms. Palmer remained with Alex. She looked truly upset. "I'm sorry that you've become the face of this controversy. You did make the correct choice."

"I know, but that doesn't change how kids are acting."

"Let time work its magic," Ms. Palmer advised. "Something else will come along and they will all move on. People have short memories."

Alex pointed to the wall behind her, decorated with football game posters and pennants. "Maybe in the rest of America people have short memories, but I think it will take something major to distract Ashland, Texas, from football."

CHAPTER EIGHT

"Are you ready to play football?" Coach Kenerson barked as Ava jogged onto the field.

"Always ready, Coach!" she called back.

"You don't look ready." He tilted his head, peering suspiciously at her face.

"Fast feet and steady hands." Ava ran in place and raised her free hand. In her other hand she grasped her helmet.

Coach K paused as if about to say something, then merely grunted. "Join the others and give me thirty push-ups."

Ava couldn't believe she'd gotten away with coming to practice with this much makeup on. The girl volleyball players were forced to scrub their faces in the locker room. For once, being the only girl worked in her favor. Coach K clearly had yet to formulate rules about eyeliner and mascara on his field.

The day had gone surprisingly well, despite how ridiculous she felt. Whenever she saw Owen, she turned on the high-pitched giggles. Everything was *oh so* funny! Kylie had missed lunch to take a makeup quiz, and Ava and Alex had sat together at a small table near Owen. They loudly discussed the pros and cons of getting highlights and ranked their favorite stores at the mall.

The conversation made Ava twitch. Owen must be repulsed by her by now, right?

But she had to be completely sure.

"Hey, Miss Fancy Pants!" Xander crowed.

Ava ignored him and the stupid comments the other boys tossed out, as Coach K paired them up for passing and receiving drills. He kept Corey and Owen together and put Ava with Kal Tippett.

Kal scowled at her. "Hey, Coach, I need a new partner. What if Ava breaks a nail?"

Ava gritted her teeth as the boys' eyes all zeroed in on her newly polished sparkly red nails. She had plenty of biting comebacks ready for Kal, but she held her tongue, because Owen stood nearby. Instead she giggled.

"Tippett, just throw the ball." Coach K eyed her again. "And Sackett—catch it."

Ava wasn't sure how far to go with this help-less girly-girl routine. She didn't want Coach Kenerson forgetting she was as tough as any of the guys on the field. She wondered if she should confide in him. Explain how she was pushing off Owen so he could focus on catching the ball. Let him in on the plan. But she couldn't read his eyes though the lenses of his mirrored sunglasses as he paced the sideline. She feared she'd come off looking even sillier than she was acting.

It's all for the good of the team, she reminded herself each time she forced herself to giggle and fumble the ball when Owen's gaze traveled her way. As soon as he turned back, she threw herself at the ball, completing the most amazing catches.

Drop, giggle.

Leap and catch.

I can't keep doing this, she thought. She was confusing even herself. *Time for the secret weapon.*

"Can I grab a drink?" she asked Coach MacDonald.

"Make it quick," he replied.

Ava hurried to the bench and fished inside her gym bag until her fingers wrapped around a small glass bottle. Turning away from the field, Ava pulled it out. One . . . two . . . three huge spritzes.

She fought back a gag as a heavy blanket of lavender perfume settled on her. Whew! That was strong! *One more for good luck.* She gave her neck another huge spray.

"Huddle up!" Corey called, waving the players to him.

Ava jogged over and wriggled her way into the circle, standing purposely next to Owen. He recoiled at the smell of her.

"Does anyone smell that?" he asked.

"It's coming from Ava," Kal reported. He was on her other side.

"You reek, Sackett!" Xander said.

"You don't like it?" she said innocently, playing it up because none of the coaches were in their huddle.

"You smell like my grandma when she gets all dressed up for a funeral!" Ryan cried.

"It's making my eyes burn," Owen complained. "I can hardly breathe!"

"Really? I think it smells so nice. Lavender is my absolute favorite scent. I spray it almost everywhere at home," she went on.

"Have you lost your mind, Ava?" Corey demanded.

Ava shrugged. "I just wanted to smell nice."

"I'm going to barf," Owen declared, backing away from the huddle.

Perfume stink-out was working!

When Luke arrived the next night, Alex was waiting and ready in the kitchen. She'd put on a cute dress with a tiny purple-flower print and her shiny black ballet flats. Around her neck she'd draped several silver necklaces, and she'd added a sparkly clip to her hair.

She busied herself slicing an avocado for her lunch the next day. Her dad and Tommy had gone back to the high school to review game film for Friday's matchup against the Cleary Titans. Mrs. Sackett was out in the garage, working on her pottery.

Alex secretly watched Luke as he sat next to Ava to review her math problems. Pieces of his sandy hair poked out from the sides of his Astros baseball cap. *So cute!*

"So what happened with the football dude?" Luke asked.

"I thought I'd scared him away." Ava explained yesterday's Operation Girly-Girl, and Luke laughed at the perfume attack. "But today, when I came to school in slightly more normal clothes, he was back to giving me goofy grins again. Yesterday was a waste."

"It was a first step. You need to go at it stronger," Luke advised.

"Stronger how?" Alex jumped in. She moved closer so he'd be sure to see how pretty she looked.

"More high maintenance," Luke explained. "More off-the-charts diva."

"I don't think I can do that," Ava confided.

"Listen, I'm exactly like Owen. I can't stand girls who are obsessed with fashion and silly drama. I like a natural girl who doesn't freak out if she gets dirty. Ava, you've got to act like the polar opposite to drive him away." He turned to Alex. "Right, Alex?"

"Right," she agreed. Then she stared down in horror at her cutesy dress. He didn't like girls who were into fashion? He liked the natural look?

She'd been going about this all wrong!

CHAPTER NINE

Ava flopped onto her bed. If Luke hadn't shown up tonight, there was no way she would've been able to finish her homework. Everything was such a mess!

She gazed down at her phone resting in her palm, hoping for a message from Kylie.

Nothing.

Should I try her again? she wondered.

Kylie had avoided her at school the last two days, meeting with teachers during lunch and avoiding her in the halls. Ava had texted a million apologies. She'd even tucked a note in her friend's locker.

But Kylie stayed silent. And Ava felt worse and worse.

If we'd been friends longer, then Kylie would know that I'm not a backstabber, she thought. *I would never hurt my friends.*

Ava dug her laptop out from under a pile of sweatshirts and pajamas. She logged on to the school e-mail portal.

Nothing from Kylie.

She clicked on a message marked *Important* from Logan Medina.

SIGN OUR PETITION TO GET BACK THE SCOREBOARD appeared on her screen.

Ava quickly read the document. A bunch of football players had banded together to convince the school's administration to overturn the student council's decision. They wanted what was promised to them. And they wanted Ava to sign their petition.

She quickly counted the signatures. Thirty-four. That was a lot.

She kind of agreed that they were owed the scoreboard, but she would never do that to Alex. She wasn't going to sign it. Sisters always came first.

She wondered if Alex knew about the petition. Her bedroom door had been closed when Ava had come upstairs.

Her phone buzzed, and Ava sat up. *Is that Kylie?*

No, it was Jack.

How's your boyfriend?

Ava groaned.

I do not have a boyfriend!!!

Not what I hear.

You heard wrong!!!

Football guys say you do. Owen!

They're so wrong!

She didn't want Jack thinking she and Owen were a couple. Jack was the one she liked hanging out with. Was Owen going to mess that up too?

Ava's eyes returned to the petition, still open on her screen. Even though she wasn't going to sign it, she felt like she should do something to stop it. But what?

Ava left her room in search of Alex. Alex's

door now lay open. The door of the small bathroom they shared was closed, and she heard the drumming of the shower.

Ava pounded on the bathroom door.

"I'll be out in a minute!" Alex yelled back.

Ava snorted. *That* wasn't true. Alex would be in there for at least twenty minutes, deep-conditioning her long hair. Ava considered barging in and talking through the striped shower curtain as she often did, but she knew Alex hated that. She'd find her mom instead. She would know how to handle the petition.

"Are you in here?" she called when she entered the garage. Her mom's potter's wheel, kiln, and drying racks of finished pots took up one side. The other side overflowed with boxes and rolls of bubble wrap, along with the lawn mower, bikes, and random sports equipment.

"Always," her mom called from behind a tall stack of boxes.

Ava spotted her mother cross-legged on the floor, attaching shipping labels.

"I need to wrap all the pieces, then pack and seal the boxes to get them to the post office tomorrow." Her hair fell into her face, and she brushed it away. "I have a rhythm going. If I keep at it, I'll get it done. Everything okay, pumpkin?"

Ava hesitated. She didn't want to bother her mom while she was so busy.

Her phone, which she had carried out with her, buzzed. Probably Jack again. "Well," she started, about to offer to help write labels, when she noticed the name on the screen. *Kylie!*

"All's good now!" Ava ducked back into the house. She sat on the sofa in the dark family room, not bothering to turn on any lights, to read Kylie's long text.

Kylie now believed that Ava truly didn't like Owen. Plus, she missed her best friend.

Ava had missed her, too.

Ava texted her back and explained to her how Alex had found out all the things Owen didn't like, Luke's plan, and her makeover.

Your crazy outfit! I had no idea what that was about. Sorry, but bad plan. You need to tell him outright.

That feels harsh.

It's not fair to let him think you like

him or want the bracelet. He's a
nice guy. You be nice too!

Ava stretched out on the sofa, considering. She didn't want to hurt Owen, yet she knew Kylie was right. Telling him the truth was the only way.

Alex emerged from the bathroom in her pink robe and matching slippers, with her wet hair pulled into two braids. In the morning, when she undid the braids, her waves would fall perfectly.

"Ave? What's up with the pounding?" she called, poking her head into her twin's bedroom.

Ava wasn't there. Alex shook her head. Ava's bedroom was such a disaster! Clothes everywhere. Smelly sneakers and sports magazines. An empty bag of chips. Alex and her mom had worked so hard to paint and decorate Ava's room in complementary blues, greens, and corals, but the effect was lost with the colossal mess.

Ava couldn't understand why her mess bothered Alex if she didn't sleep there, but it did. Alex entered and tossed the chip bag in the trash. She reached to straighten Ava's comforter, bumping her laptop, which was wedged by a pile of pajamas. The heading on the screen screamed out at her.

A petition for the scoreboard? Alex pulled the laptop closer. Her mouth dropped open as she counted all the signatures. So many! She read the note the players had sent to Ava: WE MUST STICK TOGETHER NO MATTER WHAT. OUR TEAM IS OUR FAMILY.

Ava hadn't responded. She hadn't said, *No way.* She hadn't said, *My sister is my family, and she made the right choice.* Instead she'd left the page open. As if she were thinking about it. As if she were going to sign.

Alex wanted to cry and scream all at the same time. How could football be more important to Ava than Alex?

She hurried downstairs to find her mom. She would set Ava straight.

She raced by the darkened family room, through the kitchen, and out into the garage.

"Argh!" her mother cried out, more to herself than to Alex.

"Everything okay?" Alex asked. Her mom held half of a ceramic vase in each hand. Unless her mom was trying out some sort of modern art, it seemed like the vase was broken.

"No, everything's not okay," Mrs. Sackett said simply. She blew several stray strands of hair from her tired eyes. Sheets of bubble wrap puddled at her feet. "I'm moving too fast, and now I've broken this."

"You should slow down," Alex offered.

"There's no time. I need to ship this all out and then start on the next round of orders."

"But it's good to have all the orders, right?" Alex tried to raise her mom's spirits. "You're a success!"

"Yes, it is. Very good. I just feel bad that I have no time for you or your sister or brother lately."

"That's okay. We're fine." Alex didn't feel fine, but she couldn't tell her mom right now. "Do you want me to help?"

"No, honey. I've got it. Do you mind if I say good night to you here and don't come upstairs for a kiss?"

"Sure." Alex kissed her mom and trudged back to her bedroom. Her dad and Tommy were still out. She had no idea where Ava was, and she didn't feel like looking for her. Or talking with her.

She slid under her comforter, feeling very alone.

CHAPTER TEN

Ava considered the sky the next morning. Was this a Texas thing? It looked as if a child had colored it in with a yellow-green crayon instead of blue.

All the students' eyes stayed fixed on their phone screens or held that unfocused, early morning glaze as they moved from the bus into the front doors of the middle school. No one but her looked up.

Alex would probably know what it meant, but for some reason, she'd gotten a ride early from their dad. Today was high school game day, and they'd left before Ava had rolled out of bed. Without Alex's help, she hadn't bothered dressing up at all for Owen. She'd thrown on a sweatshirt and jeans.

On the bus, Ava debated telling him she had another boyfriend. A guy from back home—that had worked for Alex, for a while, at least.

But as she entered the school and felt the little jewelry box in her pocket, she knew she should listen to Kylie. She had to stop playing games and be truthful.

Now.

Before tomorrow's football game.

She quickly spotted Owen's dark curly hair down the hall. She pushed her way forward, hoping to reach him before classes started.

"Watch it, Ava!" Alex stood before her, her lips pressed tightly into a grim line.

"Sorry, Al! Did I bump you?" Ava waved to Logan and Xander.

Alex glared at her.

"Hey, what's wrong?" Ava asked.

"Why do you care?"

"Huh?" Ava craned her neck, trying to keep Owen in sight.

"You have your team to stick with you." Alex walked off without looking back.

Ava blinked. What did *that* mean? Was Alex

angry? About what? She couldn't recall them having a fight last night.

The bell rang, sending everyone, including Owen, scurrying to their first-period classes. She wouldn't see him again until fourth-period math, their first class together. But as soon as Ava entered Mrs. Vargas's room, the teacher passed out a pop quiz and announced there was to be no talking.

Another chance gone, Ava realized, although slightly grateful for the quiz because Bridget, now wearing the kitten top from Spruce and a confused expression about Ava's transformation back to her comfy clothes, looked as if she had a lot to say.

Ava didn't want to explain her scheme to Bridget. Not yet.

Later, as she sat in Mrs. Hyde's office, listening to the learning specialist go over the answers to the quiz, Ava reviewed her options.

She hadn't been able to get to Owen after class. She was missing lunch to meet with Mrs. Hyde. But lunch was too public a place to give Owen back the bracelet anyhow. That left football practice. She had to find him outside the locker room. Talking to him in front of the other guys would be humiliating for both of them.

During the final class of the day, she watched out the window as the sky changed to a greenish-gray and rain began to fall heavily. She knew her dad would be looking out a window in the high school, too, frustrated that his team would have to play in this weather.

The rain increased and the sky boomed with thunder as the school day came to an end. Mrs. Gusman came on the loudspeaker. "All after-school activities are canceled today due to the weather, with the exception of football. Football will have practice in the south gym."

Figures, Ava thought. *Coach K would never let us miss a day of training. At least I can still find Owen before the weekend.*

She waited by the locker-room doors, searching for him as the other students filed out of the building onto buses and into waiting cars. She wondered if Alex was on the bus.

All the boys greeted her as they entered the locker room. She pretended she was in the hall answering important texts. Owen was the last to appear.

"Hi!" she called, intercepting him. Thankfully, he was alone. Her heart beat quickly.

"Hi." His eyes moved toward her bare wrist.

Ava's phone buzzed, but she ignored it. She felt more nervous than she'd felt walking into Ashland Middle School on her first day. She stood awkwardly in front of him. Now what?

"Can you believe we're the only ones still in the school?" she asked, unsure how to begin.

"Crazy," Owen agreed.

Her phone buzzed again and again. She glanced at the screen. Her dad. She'd read his texts later. She had to do this before she chickened out. She took a deep breath and reached into her pocket for the box. *Okay,* she told herself. *Here goes.*

"Listen, I—" At that moment, a siren blared.

Ava startled. It didn't sound like the fire alarm.

"I wanted to—" she started again, but the siren blared again.

"All students still in the building report immediately to the office," announced the principal over the crackling loudspeaker. "I repeat: All students proceed *immediately* to the office. This is *not* a drill."

Ava stood frozen, her hand still wrapped around the little box. Boys streamed out of the locker room.

"Come on!" Owen called, nudging her into motion. He darted toward the office, as the siren continued to blare. Ava's phone rang and rang, blending in with the siren.

"What's happening?" she cried, hurrying along-side him.

"Tornado!" Owen explained. "A tornado is coming! That's the siren."

"W-what?" Ava said, shouting above the noise.

Her phone wouldn't stop buzzing and ringing. Texts from her father. He and Tommy were leaving the high school. Mrs. Sackett was already on her way to pick up her and Alex.

Alex? Was Alex still in the school? Where? Ava thought only the football team was left.

Ava pushed into the crowded office. Mrs. Gusman and Coach K were taking attendance. They explained that if anyone's parents couldn't get there in time, they would all go to the school's safe room together to wait out the tornado. The other kids, mostly the boys on the team with her, seemed calm. They'd all grown up with tor-nado drills.

But she hadn't.

All she could picture was Dorothy in her fly-ing house spinning in the sky. She whipped her neck around, searching for Alex. The safe room would only feel safe with her twin by her side. Alex was always good in a crisis.

But Alex wasn't here. Where was she?

At that moment, her mom raced through the doors. No clay in her hair. No longer wearing the sweats she'd been working in all week. Clad in a rain slicker and high-top rain boots, her mom wore a determined look that Ava knew meant business.

Ava's mom pushed her way toward Mrs. Gusman. "I'm signing out Ava and Alex Sackett."

Over her mom's shoulder, Ava spied Alex standing in the hall alongside Ms. Palmer.

"We need to go now," Mrs. Sackett said, leading them toward the parking lot. The rain had slowed, and the air was hot and sticky.

"But look over there." Ava pointed to a patch of sunlit sky in the distance. Maybe her mom was overreacting. After all, she'd grown up in Massachusetts. Tornadoes were foreign to them. Ava scanned the gray sky. No funnel, just heavy clouds and a slight drizzle.

"Hurry up, Ava!" Mrs. Sackett prodded, as Alex climbed into the front seat.

As they exited the lot, a line of cars streamed

in to pick up the waiting students. Every other parent had the same sense of urgency.

"A tornado touched down in Stirling. That's about a half hour away," their mom reported. "The radio says more are coming."

She stepped on the gas.

Alex chewed her thumbnail as Mrs. Sackett wove through the suburban Texas streets toward home. The sky grew increasingly dark and the winds picked up. The single patch of sunlight disappeared. Strangely, the rain stopped completely.

Ava kept asking her questions about tornadoes from the backseat, but Alex pretended to be too busy watching the swirling debris lifting from the curb to respond. She *had* watched a lot of disaster shows on the Geography Channel, but right now she didn't feel like talking.

She was still angry and hurt. Her mind stayed on the scoreboard controversy.

Ms. Palmer hadn't known about the petition until Alex had told her, but that didn't mean that the football players wouldn't give it to the principal. Or ask for Logan to replace her.

And Ava still hadn't said anything to her about it. That meant she was hiding something. Had she signed it?

"Oh my!" Mrs. Sackett hit the brakes as a flattened cardboard box flew across the road and bounced off the windshield.

"Mom, keep driving!" Alex said. "We're much safer at home than out here on the open road."

"I know." Her mom picked up speed, her eyes tracking the lawn signs and garbage bags tumbling about. The wind rattled the windows of the car.

"Tommy just texted." Ava poked her head forward. "He and Daddy are almost at Saragaso Way."

"I wish they were with us," Mrs. Sackett said quietly.

Alex turned on the radio. The announcers on the local stations sounded serious as they tracked the storm. They all agreed: The tornado was heading toward Ashland!

"Please, turn down the volume. They're freaking me out." Ava twirled a pen in her fingers. "Will we make it home?"

"Sure," Mrs. Sackett said, her voice wavering slightly.

Alex made a list in her head. Lists always calmed her. They gave life order. She calculated the distance they had to drive and the speed of the wind. But then there were other variables— temperature and pressure systems and other things the weather forecasters always said. It was like one of those hard math word problems, and the numbers didn't add up.

She realized with a shudder that she couldn't make order out of a tornado.

All she could do was hope and pray that they made it home before it touched down.

CHAPTER ELEVEN

Ava let out a whoop as their car pulled into the driveway only seconds behind Coach's. Everyone tumbled out and sprinted into the house, the wind whipping their hair into knots.

"Tommy, make sure all the windows are locked and shut the shades," Mrs. Sackett commanded above the roar of the wind. "And then everyone stay far away from the windows in case they shatter."

Ava reached down to calm Moxy, who circled her, panting and whimpering. "Moxy's not happy."

"She's a smart dog," Coach said, helping Tommy secure the house.

"Put Moxy on a leash to keep her close," Mrs.

Sackett instructed, then ran into the kitchen. She returned with flashlights. "Everyone into the bathroom. Now!"

"The bathroom? All of us?" Alex asked. The downstairs bathroom off the kitchen was tiny.

"Yes," her mom said. "I've read up on this. A small interior room with no windows is the safest spot."

"One sec. I'm going upstairs," Tommy announced as the branches of the tree along-side the house scraped loudly against the siding. "Got to save my keyboard."

"Oh, no! We're all staying downstairs together." Coach Sackett grabbed the back of Tommy's shirt and pulled him into the bath-room. The lights in the house flickered.

"We're not going to fit," Ava complained.

"You and Alex squeeze in the tub," Mrs. Sackett said. "Bring Moxy, too. Be right back!"

"Laura!" their dad called as the lights went out.

"Hold on, Dorothy, we're in for a ride!" Tommy joked. He snapped on a flashlight.

Ava pulled her knees to her chin inside the white ceramic bathtub. Moxy pressed her trem-bling body against her, her damp fur tickling

Ava's nose. Alex squeezed beside her in the same Buddha-like position, her back angled away, nose-to-nose with the faucet.

"Are you okay?" Ava had felt a strange cold-ness between them the whole ride home.

"Do I look okay?" Alex shot back.

None of them looked okay. Tommy huddled on the closed toilet, and Coach was pressed against the towel bar. Mrs. Sackett hurried in, closed the door tightly behind her, and squeezed against the sink. Not an inch of space remained. The single beam of Tommy's flashlight bounced along the sage-green walls.

"What's in there?" Tommy pointed to the huge, lumpy sack Mrs. Sackett had dragged in.

She reached inside and pulled out five foot-ball helmets.

"Team sports?" Tommy laughed. "I never knew you wanted to play, Mom."

"I don't," Mrs. Sackett replied. "The helmets are to keep our heads safe."

"Safe from what?" Ava asked.

"The tornado." Their mom handed each of them a banged-up helmet. "I know I've been wrapped up in my work, but I put it on hold to go into preparation mode this morning. I bought milk, bread, batteries, and cases of water. And I came up with the helmet idea. We certainly have enough of them in the garage."

"I'm not wearing this!" Alex protested, sniffing the inside. "It reeks like Tommy's smelly feet."

Tommy pushed his big feet onto the rim of the tub, and both girls swatted them away.

"It's too tight in here for that nonsense," Coach said. "Listen to your mother. Suit up."

They all slipped on the helmets and waited silently, as the roar of the wind increased and the tornado closed in. Ava felt her insides tighten. Her parents gave her stiff smiles from behind the grilles of their helmets. But their false grins didn't mask their worry. Her dad reached for her mom's hand.

"Remember how we used to hold hands during thunderstorms?" Ava whispered to Alex, who sat rigid next to her with her helmet sagging over her eyes.

When they were little, they would intertwine their fingers, squeezing and daring each other to let go. Letting go first meant you lost.

"You should've stayed with your football family. I bet they would hold your hand," Alex muttered. "You guys stick together, right?"

"Stay with them? What are you talking about?" Ava asked.

"Girls, not now, okay?" Coach asked. He gazed uncertainly at the ceiling.

Moxy wiggled and tried to stand. Ava pushed her down uncomfortably into her lap. Alex crossed her arms and stared stonily at the drain, refusing to speak.

With the bobbing beam of the flashlight, the scary rush of wind, and Moxy's damp-dog stench, the bathroom felt as if it were growing smaller and smaller.

"What is your problem?" Ava finally demanded. She was never able to outlast Alex's silent treatment.

"I know you chose them over me," Alex said quietly.

"Who?" Ava couldn't make sense of her sister's words.

"Girls, this is not the time to bicker," Mrs. Sackett said, her voice barely audible.

"Look." Alex leaned over Moxy's head. "I know you signed that petition. I can't believe you chose your team over your twin."

"What?" Ava cried. "I—"

The rest of her words were drowned out by

what sounded like a jumbo jet touching down on their roof. The roar momentarily shook the house.

Instinctively, Ava reached for Alex's hand. Alex hesitated, then held on tight, and they squeezed their fingers together.

Neither letting go.

As fast as the roar came, it left. They all huddled together, listening to one another breathe in the sudden silence. Alex heard her heart thudding.

Tommy waved his flashlight from face to face. "That was weird."

"That was scary," Mrs. Sackett corrected.

"I think it passed through," Coach added.

Alex felt Ava's warm fingers still laced with hers. She liked how perfectly they fit together. "Did you sign?" she asked softly.

"I didn't. I would *never* sign," Ava replied.

Alex blinked back her surprise and the rush of relief. "But you worked so hard to be a part of the team."

"Do you seriously think I'd choose a scoreboard over you?" Ava asked.

"I hoped not, but it seems as if everyone is against me."

"Not everyone."

"What are you two going on about?" Tommy demanded.

"It's a twin thing," Alex and Ava said at the same time. They shared a secret smile.

"Can we get out of here?" Tommy asked.

"Let's go," Mrs. Sackett agreed. She pushed open the door. Moxy leaped up and trotted into the dark house.

Alex stood in the tub, hand in hand with Ava. Football helmets still on, they stepped out together to survey the damage.

CHAPTER TWELVE

Alex parted the curtains in the family room and stared out at the empty street. The rain had together started up again and the wind, although greatly lessened, still swayed the trees. Branches and twigs littered their lawn. No one was outside. The town felt eerily silent.

Would another tornado follow? Sometimes that happened, she knew.

The house looked the same as it always had, except the lights, TV, and phone didn't work. She glanced at her phone. "How can it only be four o'clock?" The ride home and the huddle in the bathroom felt as if it had lasted a lifetime.

"No game tonight," Coach said, sending the

announcement out through his cell phone.

"Really?" Ava asked. "Because our team looks ready to take the field."

Alex laughed. They all still wore their helmets! What would Johnny from student council think if he could see her now? The Sacketts really were all about football!

"Friday night and no game," Tommy muttered, pulling off his helmet. "Can I go to Luke's?"

"No way," their mom said. "You're staying put until we're sure this weather has passed."

"What are we going to do here with no power?" Tommy grimaced. "You know, if I had a real piano instead of an electric keyboard, I'd be able to play it now. Wouldn't that be nice?"

"Nice try," Coach said. "Not happening."

"Thought it was worth a shot." Tommy had been angling for a piano ever since they'd moved.

"I know! Game night!" Alex cried. She loved board games. She didn't stand a chance out on a field with her father, Tommy, and Ava, but board games were her thing. And her mom's, too, but Alex was way more competitive. She grabbed a flashlight and pulled her favorites from the shelves. Coach lit candles and they all gathered around the table.

"Kylie just texted. Her family is fine. And Jack texted that they're all good too," Ava reported.

"Phones away," Alex commanded. "You too, Daddy."

"Did that tornado rattle your brain?" Tommy asked. "The Queen of Texting is asking us to power down?"

"You'll all need your full attention if you have any chance against me in these games!" Alex crowed, turning off her phone.

After several rounds of Apples to Apples, Scrabble, and Clue, Tommy gave up. "I'm losing because I'm hungry."

"That's a lame excuse," Alex replied. "You're always hungry."

"Actually, hungry is good. Very good," Coach said. "We need Tommy to devour the food in the fridge and freezer. Without power, it'll melt or go bad."

"Oh no!" Mrs. Sackett jumped up. "Everyone follow me!"

They trailed her into the garage. Even Moxy followed. Mrs. Sackett pulled open the freezer door of the extra refrigerator in the corner.

"Is that all ice cream?" Alex asked. Forty cartons were stacked inside. Chocolate, vanilla, cookie dough, peanut butter fudge swirl . . . She couldn't read all the different flavors.

"The Ice Cream Chow-Down. Wow! It's tonight. Or I guess it was supposed to be." Coach scratched his head.

"Are you surprised I remembered?" their mom asked.

"Well, you have been a bit preoccupied lately . . . ," Coach started.

"You shouldn't doubt me," she teased.

"You're so right." He groaned. "But for once, I decided not to bother you with the team. I called the Creamery yesterday. They're scheduled to deliver twenty gallons of ice cream to the house later!"

"More ice cream?" Alex cried.

"And we're not even having all those guys over," Ava added.

"There's still going to be an ice cream chow-down tonight, just with a different team. The Sackett team. Ava, go grab five spoons," Mrs. Sackett said. "Everyone pick a flavor. We need to eat as much of this as we can before it melts!"

"And before the ice cream truck arrives," Coach Sackett added. "I don't think I can cancel the delivery."

Alex reached for the cherry vanilla. She gazed at the pots and bowls on the drying rack. Her mom had run out this morning to buy the ice cream and prepare them for the storm when she should have been getting the ceramics ready to ship.

"I have an idea," she announced, and in minutes she formed everyone into an assembly line. Sharing ice cream straight from the cartons, they wrapped, packed, and labeled by candlelight.

Tommy popped the bubble wrap as they worked. "Name that tune," he said.

"'Row, Row, Row Your Boat,'" Alex guessed. Tommy was forever tapping out tunes on odd objects.

"No! It's 'Yellow Rose of Texas.'" Tommy scowled and tried to pick out the notes again.

"What's that song?" Ava asked, sticking her spoon into the peanut butter fudge swirl.

"Only the best Texas song ever," Coach said. Then he began to sing. His voice was deep and very flat.

"No!" Alex and Ava teased, plugging their ears.

"You want to talk Texas?" Their father didn't wait for an answer and launched into a story of a huge storm he'd been through when he was growing up in Texas.

The hum of the refrigerator suddenly filled the air, and the lights turned back on. Ava cheered, but Alex felt a bit let down. Having the tornado come through Ashland had been strangely fun. She loved having her family laughing and talking together on a Friday night. When was the last time that had happened during football season? Had it ever happened during football season?

Moxy barked and paced in front of the side door that led into the garage.

"Knock, knock!" called a man's deep voice.

Her dad opened the door to find Doug Kelly, their neighbor, on the stoop. Mr. Kelly, whose son PJ was the high school quarterback, had broad shoulders and a hulking frame that made Alex suspect he'd played Texas football when he was in school.

"You folks all right?" Mr. Kelly asked, pushing his thick, graying hair from his eyes. "Figured I'd walk about and check up on y'all."

"That's mighty kind of you," Coach said. "We're fine. Your family?"

Mr. Kelly nodded. "This section of town fared okay. Some downed branches and a missing shingle or two, but that's nothing. But I'm hearing reports that over at the middle school—"

"Is everyone okay?" Alex jumped in. She thought of all the kids waiting for their parents when she and Ava had left with their mom.

"All the kids and teachers took cover long before it hit. The warning was early this time," Mr. Kelly said. "It's the football field and the baseball diamond. The twister churned them up something good."

"Churned them up?" Ava asked.

"The tornado missed the school buildings but bulldozed its way down the fields. Trees are uprooted. The bleachers are in pieces, and the scoreboard splintered. One goalpost is leaning. And grass and dirt are everywhere," he said.

"But we have a big game tomorrow," Ava cried.

Mr. Kelly shook his head. "Not on that field, you don't. The game's been canceled. I have no idea where the middle school will play or practice for the next few weeks. They say the field is destroyed." Alex couldn't tell if he was happy or sad about this. He had tried to prevent Ava from getting on the football team; he was one of the people who didn't think girls should play.

Ava's eyes grew wide. "But we were just starting our season."

Alex felt horrible for Ava. And for the team.

True, they hadn't been so nice to her lately, but they'd been upset about losing their new scoreboard. She got that, even though she didn't agree with them. And now they'd lost their home field. Alex knew that was a big deal. Her dad always told her teams played better on the grass they knew and practiced on.

She wished she could find them a new field. But where? She'd only just moved to Ashland. She knew nothing about fields.

Mr. Kelly changed the conversation to the high school team's prospects, and Alex tuned out. She placed the final box on top of the pile of boxes that were labeled, packed, and ready to ship. She was proud they'd banded together today to help her mom. Then she thought back to the drama club's flood. The student council had banded together to buy them new costumes and props.

Maybe they could do the same for the football team.

She grabbed a piece of paper and a pen. She needed to make a list. And turn her phone back on.

They didn't need a new field.

She was going to fix the old one.

CHAPTER THIRTEEN

Alex tapped her clipboard with her purple pen and squinted into the Sunday afternoon sun at the football field.

"Your text blasts really worked," Chloe Klein remarked. "All of Ashland is here."

Alex couldn't get over all the people who'd shown up. Parents, teachers, middle school kids, high school kids, even little kids.

"We need to get all these folks working," Ms. Palmer said to the student council, who stood together wearing red shirts.

"Watch this." Johnny Morton placed two fingers in his mouth and let out an ear-piercing whistle. Everyone turned. "It's your show," he said to Alex.

"Oh, no! This is a student council thing," Alex said. "All of us."

"Yeah, you've said that before," Johnny said. "But you took the heat for the scoreboard. You should get props for this great idea."

"Come on, Alex." Chloe nudged her forward. "You already made all those lists."

Alex gazed at the papers on her clipboard. She'd spent the last twenty-four hours calling the local hardware, lumber, and garden stores and asking for donations. She'd surprised herself. She was a pretty good salesperson. She'd gotten tractors, topsoil, grass seed and sod, wood, tools, and lots of trash bags. Then again, as Tommy pointed out, she was selling football in Texas, which was easier than selling ice cream to a hungry child on a hot summer day.

Alex didn't care. This was what she liked about being an elected official. Helping people.

She blushed and turned to Mayor Johnston. He was the real elected official here. "You should speak," she said.

"Nonsense, Alex." But his ruddy face broke into a grin. He proudly introduced her and the rest of the student council to the crowd.

Alex thanked everyone for their generous

help. With Ms. Palmer's guidance, she divided them into groups. Johnny handed out garbage bags to the middle school kids. The high school kids started clearing the field. Her dad, Mayor Johnston, Coach K, and a bunch of parents began to dismantle the mangled bleachers.

Girls on the dance team taught the younger kids line dances. Hordes of people waited by tables piled high with sweets to buy Coach Sackett's famous chocolate chip blondies and cherry crumble. Folks loved the idea of their big, athletic football coach in an apron. He'd spent all day yesterday in the kitchen. Next to the bake sale, her mom had set up a table with a new batch of ceramic pots, which she'd glazed in Ashland football colors. Several other parents and local stores had also put up tables. Alex was sure they'd be able to raise enough money for the new bleachers and scoreboard.

The sun was high in the blue sky, and the field bustled as if they were at a carnival, not a tornado cleanup.

"Where is he?" Emily asked, coming up with Lindsey behind Alex.

"Who?" She looked toward the battered ticket booth. The cast of *The Wizard of Oz* was in full costume, charging parents to have their kids take a photo with Dorothy and her friends. Spencer the Scarecrow danced about, and the kids all wanted to pet the little dog that played Toto.

"Your high school guy," Lindsey prodded. "Is he a football player?"

Their eyes traveled to the concession stand, where the football team was about to start the Ice Cream Chow-Down to raise money. People were betting to see which linebacker could out-eat the other. The cheerleaders had created the largest sundaes Alex had ever seen!

"No, he's not on the team. That would be too weird with my dad and all," Alex said. She wished she'd never told them about Luke. She knew there wasn't anything really to tell. Yet.

"So true," Lindsey agreed. "He is here, right?"

Luke was watching Tommy and his jazz trio perform back by the baseball diamond. A crowd of kids surrounded them. She pointed at Luke clapping along to the beat, his sandy curls covering his eyes. "That's him."

"Wow." Emily's eyes widened.

"He's so cute," Lindsey agreed. "Can we go say hi?"

"No!" She hadn't meant to shout. "I mean, not

now. He seems really into the show, and oh, hey, the bake sale needs more help. Do you guys mind?"

Alex breathed a sigh of relief as they hurried off to sell cookies. She hadn't even said hi to Luke yet. She'd been too busy—and too nervous. Somewhere in the distance she heard Johnny, then her mom, call her name, but she didn't answer. Instead she stood with her clipboard, watching Luke.

Wishing he'd look up and notice her.

Ava placed a piece of crumpled notebook paper in her plastic garbage bag, but her eyes stayed on Owen. She'd been watching him for an hour. Now he joked with Logan as they gathered twigs.

She tried to mentally will Logan away, but the boy wouldn't budge from Owen's side.

She glanced down at the crumpled science notes in blue ink. *How did someone's science notes get blown onto the field?* she wondered.

The tornado had done some weird things. In the nearby town of Roscoe, where the twister had hit the hardest, several hay bales went flying and landed on top of the church's pointy spire!

As she bent forward to grab more debris, she was aware once again of the little box with the delicate silver bracelet in the pocket of her thin hoodie. It felt like a twenty-pound boulder. All day Ava had kept to herself, avoiding Jack and Kylie. She couldn't laugh or talk with them.

She needed to do this. *Now*. She'd waited far too long.

"Owen!" she called. "Can we talk?"

Logan smirked. "Ohhh! K-I-S-S-I-N-G," he sang.

"Grow up, Medina," Ava scoffed. She motioned Owen over.

"H-hi," she stammered, once again feeling uncertain around him. "That was scary. The sirens. The tornado."

"Yeah," he agreed awkwardly. "And I've lived here forever. You must have freaked out."

"Totally." Ava babbled nervously about squeezing into the bathtub. Then she paused and pulled the little box from her pocket. "Look, I didn't want to talk about the weather."

"I kind of figured," he said, looking away from her and squinting into the distance.

"You did?" She couldn't hide her surprise.

He shrugged. "You don't really like me. You made that pretty obvious."

Ava felt horrible. "Oh, no! It's not that. I mean, I don't like you in that way, but I do like you. As a friend. On the football field . . ." The words became tangled. "And this was very sweet." She nodded toward the bracelet in the box. "But I can't accept it, because—"

"No big deal." Owen cut her off and reached for the box.

"Really?" She studied his face. He didn't look too upset.

"Ava, you did everything but project it on the Super Bowl Jumbotron. It's fine. We're good."

"Really?" she said again. How could he be so into her two days ago and now act as if he didn't care? If she had known it would be this easy, she never would have paraded around school in that hideous outfit.

"Yes, really." His face went pink, and he pushed the box deep into his pocket. "I like someone else."

Ava raised her eyebrows. "Who?"

Owen's ears burned red now. "You don't know her. She doesn't go to our school."

Ava's heart broke for Kylie. Owen was already

onto another girl! For such a quiet guy, he sure moved fast.

Ava scooped a stray football from the ground and tossed it to Owen. He caught it easily and tossed it back. In a moment, they had an easy rhythm going. Toss, catch, toss, catch.

"So we're friends now?" Ava asked.

"Yeah, sure," Owen agreed, sending the ball high. He wasn't very talkative.

"Tell me about her," Ava pressed. "The girl you like."

Owen hesitated. "I don't know."

"Come on, we're friends," Ava said. She owed it to Kylie to snoop for information.

"We met online," Owen explained. "In a chat group. We've been talking all weekend since the crazy tornado. She's really cool."

"So you connected on one of your fantasy fiction forums?" Ava asked.

Owen held on to the ball and gave her a perplexed look. "How did you know I go on those?"

Busted!

"Just a lucky guess." She lifted her arms. "Throw it here. So what's her name?"

"I don't know." Owen rocketed the ball to her. "I only know her screen name: ranchergirl722."

Ava fumbled the catch. As the ball bounced on the ground, she fought back the urge to pump her fist. *Go, Kylie!*

"You know, it was wrong of me to take the bracelet and not tell you right off," she said. "I owe you for that."

"What do you mean?"

"I think I may know your mystery girl."

This has nothing to do with Luke, Alex told herself as she headed toward the band. *As a student council officer, I need to check on the music.* Music was essential to the cleanup effort.

"Watch out!" Mr. Kelly called as a shower of soil rained down. Several men were laying sod nearby. Alex gasped as flecks of dirt landed on her shirt. She hurried to wipe them off, then stopped. She was wearing ripped jeans, sneakers, and a plain red T-shirt. Her hair was pulled back into two loose braids, and she hadn't bothered with lip gloss. The dirt added to the look.

She felt grimy, and so not herself. But if this was what it took to get Luke to notice her . . .

She spotted Corey heading her way. It startled

her to see him without Lindsey by his side. Alex looked toward the bake sale table. Lindsey and Emily were still selling cookies and brownies.

Corey took long, confident steps, his red hair glimmering in the sun. Then he shot her his megawatt smile, and she felt her insides melt.

She still liked him a lot.

As much as Luke.

Maybe even more.

What's with me? she wondered. She had two crushes, and one had a girlfriend and the other barely knew she existed.

Alex smiled back. Why was Corey coming over to her now? Had Ava had it right all along? Did boys go for this natural look? Had she been wearing the wrong clothes her whole life?

"Hey, there!" Corey stood in front of her. "You're all dirty. Do you want a towel or something?"

"No." Alex acted as if it were no big deal that her skin itched under her shirt from the bits of dirt. "Doesn't bother me."

"I hate being dirty. My mom says I'm going to have to pay our water bill because I shower so much." Corey grinned. "People can't believe that about me because of football, but hey, I like to look good."

"Me too," Alex admitted. She was now officially completely confused. One boy liked one thing. One boy liked the opposite.

"So listen," Corey said, "I came over to say thank you."

"To me? Why?"

"I'm saying thank you for the whole team. This cleanup and rebuilding was your idea."

"Someone else would have probably thought of it too."

"You thought of it first and put a plan into action. Now we'll be able to practice here this week and play our game next Saturday."

Xander, Logan, Ryan, and several other football players gathered around.

"Alex is a hero," Xander announced. "If she hadn't given the scoreboard money to the drama kids, our new scoreboard would have been standing right there when the twister came through." He pointed to the far end of the field, where the old scoreboard was being lifted in pieces into the backs of several pickup trucks.

"That would've stunk if we'd put up a new one and then a day later it was smashed," Ryan agreed.

By now, most of the team had wandered over,

including Ava and Owen. Watching the easy way they talked and tossed the ball, Alex knew Ava had finally fixed everything between them.

"Well, guess what?" Alex was bursting to share her good news. "With all the donations and the money we're raising today, not only will we fix the fields, but we're going to buy the new scoreboard, too. Ms. Palmer called the company. Since it was still in the warehouse with our name on it, they're delivering it this week."

"We're going high-tech!" Corey bellowed.

A deafening cheer rose up.

Logan produced a piece of paper and tore it into tiny pieces. With a whoop, he tossed them into the air. Confetti rained on Alex's head.

"Was that your petition?" Alex asked.

"You knew about it? It was a stupid idea," Logan admitted. "We were wrong. You're a great class president, and you've proved that you're totally pro-football."

Alex grinned. It felt good to be appreciated.

"The thing is," she corrected him, "I am pro-football, but I'm also pro drama club and pro everything that's important to the kids here. Really, I'm pro Ashland Middle School."

CHAPTER FOURTEEN

The smell of fresh grass and moist dirt tickled Ava's nose as she and the team finished their first warm-up laps around the restored field on Tuesday after school.

"A new field means a new start," Coach K declared. "And what does a new scoreboard mean?"

"It means we should light it up!" they all called.

As Coach K broke them into groups, Ava motioned to Corey and Xander. "Corey, throw Owen your toughest, longest pass."

"What's up?" Corey asked suspiciously.

"I want to show you something." Ava grinned.

"What did you do to my boy, Sackett?" Xander teased.

"Nothing," she replied. "Come on. Run the play already!"

Corey sent Owen all the way downfield before letting the ball fly. Kal and Ryan moved in to block Owen, but Owen was too quick. He dodged left, then right. Then, with a leap, he snatched the ball from the air and sprinted across the touchdown line.

"He's back!" Ava declared proudly. "No more distractions."

"Run that again," Coach K called from the sidelines. Play after play, Owen's attention stayed on the ball and on Corey. He caught and ran like a star. Coach K nodded with pleasure.

"You did that?" Xander asked Ava, as they sat together on the bench.

She nodded. "For the team."

Xander turned serious. "I hope you didn't break his heart. Owen's a good guy."

"His heart is fine. Better than fine," she assured Xander. She filled him in on her awesome matchmaking skills.

The center sent the ball back to Corey. Corey pinpointed Owen, waiting for him to find open ground, and then he bulleted the ball. Owen reached up to cradle it in an easy catch, but at the final second, his head swiveled toward the new bleachers. He stumbled and his fingers grasped at air.

Once again, the football lay at his feet.

What was that? Ava whirled around and let out a loud groan.

Kylie, in bright-green jeans and a flowing yellow top, climbed the bleachers. Owen watched her movements, as if in a trance. The telltale red blush crept up his neck.

"Here we go again." Xander sounded exasperated.

"No, no!" Ava called. "I can fix this!" Even though she knew she'd get scolded for leaving the field, she ran to Kylie's side, her cleats clattering on the metal stairs.

"What are you doing up here?" Kylie asked, bewildered.

"I need to tell you two things. Good news and bad news."

"Good first, most definitely," Kylie said.

"Okay. Good news: Owen is *totally* into you." Ava paused, delighting in Kylie's wide smile. "Now for the bad news. Don't laugh, because this is serious. You can never, ever come to another practice or game again."

Ready for more
ALEX AND AVA?

Here's a sneak peek at the
next book in the It Takes Two series:

Two Steps Back

"Hello? Yes, this is Alexandra Sackett." Alex put her hand to her right ear to muffle the sounds of the food court. "Yes. I—I did? I *did*? Oh my gosh, thank you! Yes! Yes! Yes, I will! Thank you! Bye!" She clicked off her phone and stared at it in disbelief.

Her friend Emily Campbell had paused in mid-sip of her raspberry smoothie. "What's going on, Alex? Who was that?"

Alex clutched her phone with both hands as though she expected it to leap away from her. "I won," she said quietly. "I *won*?" Her voice grew stronger. "I *won*!"

"That is so awesome!" squealed Emily,

bouncing up and down in her chair. "Congratulations! Um, what did you win?"

Alex took a breath and composed herself. She looked at her friend, her green eyes shining. "That was the assistant to Marcy Maxon, the TV reporter."

"Marcy Maxon! I totally know who that is! She's a celebrity! Why did her assistant call you?"

"I won the essay contest, Em! The one for KHXA's 'Tomorrow's Reporters Today' series? I wrote an essay, and Marcy Maxon's assistant just told me that I was selected to be a kid reporter. I get to write, produce, and star in a feature story, and it's going to air next Sunday night! She said to check my e-mail, because they'll be sending me all the details."

"Alex, that is absolutely and completely amazing!" said Emily. "Everyone in Ashland watches that segment! I've never known any of the kids who've done it, though. I can't believe I know you!"

Alex beamed at her friend. She loved that Emily seemed so genuinely happy for her, and it was fun to hear Emily's enthusiastic words in her pretty Texan drawl. Ever since Emily's best friend, Lindsey Davis, had started spending most of her time with her boyfriend, Alex and Emily had grown even closer.

Emily leaped out of her chair and came around the table to give Alex a big congratulatory hug.

"What are we celebrating?" asked a voice behind them.

Alex slackened her grip on Emily and turned to see who it was. She gasped with surprise.

Luke Grabowski was standing right there between their table and the smoothie counter. He looked impossibly gorgeous in a faded black T-shirt and khaki shorts. Behind him were two of his friends that Alex didn't know. The three of them were holding paper cups from a fancy coffee place across the way, and Luke had a book under one arm. *Of course he has a book with him,* Alex thought. He was not just beautiful; he was also smart. And funny. And nice. In short, perfect.

Luke was her twin sister Ava's tutor. Alex had had a crush on him from the moment she'd first met him, but no one in the world knew it, she was positive. Well, except maybe Emily and Lindsey, because she might have mentioned to them that she had a huge crush on a high school boy.

"Oh, hi!" she said, but her voice came out all squeaky. She didn't dare look into his gorgeous blue eyes, so instead she focused her gaze on the coffee he was holding. Drinking coffee was such a high school thing. She'd never really liked it much, but she immediately resolved to add "try coffee again" to her to-do list.

"So did you guys just win the lottery?" Luke prompted. "We heard the squealing across the food court."

Alex giggled. She raised her eyes to look at Luke, and then quickly looked away, overcome with bashfulness. She wasn't usually at a loss for words. On the contrary, Ava often told her she talked way too much and too quickly, but there was something about being in the presence of a crush that made her shy and awkward. And Luke was simply too handsome to look at for too long. It was like staring at the sun or something. But she recovered enough to introduce Emily.

"Nice to meet you, Emily," Luke said, his voice as smooth as melted chocolate. "And this is Pete, and that's Brandon. We were just loading up on caffeine before we hit the books." He held up his cup of coffee. "But tell us what the big celebration is all about," he said.

"Oh, ha-ha," said Alex. "It's no big deal." She tried not to blush, although she knew she must be turning the same shade as Emily's smoothie.

Emily stepped up and saved her. "No big deal? Yeah, right! It's a *huge* deal! I was congratulating Alex because she just won an essay contest! She's going to be a kid reporter for KHXA. Marcy Maxon's *assistant* just called her!"

"Wow!" said Luke. He put an arm around Alex's shoulder and gave her a little squeeze. She gulped.

"Awesome!" said Brandon.

Alex felt herself flush even more deeply. She couldn't think of a thing to say, but she knew that it was her turn to speak. Her eyes landed on Luke's coffee. "So, um, how's your coffee?" she asked. *Lame, lame, lame. What a dumb, stupid, idiotic question.*

"I haven't tried it yet," said Luke. He took a sip and made a face. "It's actually awful," he said, after swallowing with difficulty. "I think they gave me someone else's order. It tastes like there's pumpkin spice or something in here. They put pumpkin in everything this time of year!"

"I love pumpkin spice!" said Alex quickly, and

then mentally kicked herself. What if he thought that was babyish or something?

"Here, have it then," said Luke, handing his cup to her with an easy grin. "I'll pick up a more manly drink on my way out."

"Thanks!" said Alex. *Say something, say anything, keep the conversation going.* "So, are you enjoying the book you're reading?" she asked.

"What book? Oh, this?" He held it up for them to see the cover. The title was *Circuitry*.

Alex had no clue what circuitry was.

"It's scintillating," said Luke with a grin.

Scintillating. He had such a huge vocabulary! And obviously he loved circuitry, whatever that was. Alex made a mental note to study up on the subject.

"Well, congrats again, Al. See you soon."

And he and his friends ambled off.

Belle Payton isn't a twin herself, but she does have twin brothers! She spent much of her childhood in the bleachers reading—er, cheering them on—at their football games. Though she left the South long ago to become a children's book editor in New York City, Belle still drinks approximately a gallon of sweet tea a week and loves treating her friends to her famous homemade mac-and-cheese. Belle is the author of many books for children and tweens, and is currently having a blast writing two sides to each It Takes Two story.